"Why on [...] replace[...] It's your house, after all."

Alex's gaze lingered on the heavy oil portrait of his grandfather that hung over the dining-room fireplace. "Sometimes I find that hard to believe."

His words were so quiet, he almost seemed to be speaking to himself. Paula wanted to argue, but instinctively she knew it wouldn't do any good. She'd been wrong. It wasn't his house, not in the way she understood those words. It was the Caine mansion, and right now Alex looked as if that were a heavy burden.

She frowned down at the folder in her hand. "I'll get started on this."

Alex turned toward her, seeming to shake off the clouds that surrounded him. "Thank you."

"For what? It's my job." It was hard to sound casual when her heart clenched at his closeness.

"For being here. For helping me. I'm glad you're back."

Books by Marta Perry

Love Inspired

A Father's Promise #41
Since You've Been Gone #75
Desperately Seeking Daddy #91
The Doctor Next Door #104
Father Most Blessed #128

*Hometown Heroes

MARTA PERRY

wanted to be a writer from the moment she encountered Nancy Drew, at about age eight. She didn't see publication of her stories until many years later, when she began writing children's fiction for Sunday school papers while she was a church educational director. Although now retired from that position in order to write full-time, she continues to play an active part in her church and loves teaching a class of lively fifth- and sixth-grade Sunday school students.

Marta lives in rural Pennsylvania with her husband of thirty-seven years and has three grown children. She loves to hear from readers and enjoys responding. She can be reached c/o Steeple Hill Books, 300 East 42nd Street, New York, NY 10017.

Father Most Blessed

Marta Perry

Love Inspired®

Published by Steeple Hill Books™

STEEPLE HILL BOOKS

Steeple
Hill

ISBN 0-373-87135-X

FATHER MOST BLESSED

Visit us at www.steeplehill.com

Printed in U.S.A.

For it is by grace you have been saved, through faith, and this not from yourselves: it is the gift of God—not by works, so that no one can boast.

—*Ephesians* 2:8-9

This story is dedicated with love and gratitude to the siblings and spouses who add so much richness to our lives: Pat and Ed, Bill and Molly, Herb and Barb, Gary and Arddy, and Chris. And, as always, to Brian.

Chapter One

A man who lived in a twenty-room house ought to be able to have silence when he wanted it. Alex Caine tossed his pen on the library desk and stalked to the center hallway of the Italianate mansion that had been home to the Caine family for three generations. The noise that had disrupted his work on a crucial business deal came from beyond the swinging door to the servants' area.

Frowning, he headed toward the sound, his footsteps sharp on the marble floor, and pushed through the door to the rear of the house. He'd told his ailing housekeeper to rest this afternoon, so there should have been no sound at all to disturb his concentration. But Maida Hansen, having taken care of him since the day his mother died when he was six, tended to ignore any orders she didn't want to follow.

Well, in this case she was going to listen. If he didn't find the right words for this delicate negotiation, Caine Industries might not survive for another generation. There might be no company at all to leave to his son.

He winced. What would his grandfather or his father have said to that? They'd assumed they were founding a dynasty to last a hundred years. They wouldn't look kindly on the man who presided over its demise.

The noise came from the pantry, down the hall from the kitchen. He seized the doorknob and yanked.

The figure balanced precariously on the step stool wasn't Maida. Maida had never in her life worn blue jeans or a sweatshirt proclaiming her World's Greatest Teacher. His heart stopped, and he looked at the woman he had thought he'd never see again.

"What's going on?"

She spun at the sound of his voice, wobbled and overbalanced. Her arms waved wildly to regain control, but it was too late. The step stool toppled, sending her flying toward him. Pans clattered to the floor. In an instant his arms had closed around Paula Hansen.

The breath went out of him. Carefully he set her on her feet and stepped back, clamping down on the treacherous rush of feelings. Paula—here in his house again, looking up at him with what might have been embarrassment in her sea-green eyes.

With an effort he schooled his face to polite concern and found his voice. "Paula. I didn't expect to find you here. Maida didn't tell me you were coming."

Maida's time outside her duties was her own, and she was perfectly free to have her niece stay at the housekeeper's cottage whenever she wanted to. But in the almost two years since the plane crash, since what had happened between them, Paula hadn't returned to Bedford Creek.

"She didn't tell you?" Surprise filled Paula's expressive face. She tried to mask it, turning away to right the step stool.

"No, she didn't." If he'd known Paula was on the estate, he wouldn't have betrayed shock at the sight of her. In fact, he'd probably have found a way to avoid seeing her at all.

"But I thought she…" Paula stopped, seeming to edit whatever she'd been about to say. "My school just got out for the summer yesterday, so I'm on vacation now." Again she stopped, and again he had the sense of things left unsaid.

She'd been on vacation two years ago, when she'd come to Pennsylvania to spend the summer taking care of his son. It had seemed the perfect solution. He had needed someone reliable to care for Jason until kindergarten started in the fall. His housekeeper's niece needed a summer job. Neither of them had anticipated anything else.

The June sunlight, slanting through the small panes of the pantry window, burnished the honey blond of her hair. Her hair was shorter now than the last time he'd seen her, and it fell in unruly curls around her face. Her green eyes still reflected glints of gold, and that vulnerable mouth and stubborn chin hadn't changed.

Tension jagged along his nerves as images of the last time he'd seen her invaded his mind—lightning splitting the sky outside the small plane; the brief hope the pilot would manage to land, shattered when the plane cartwheeled and flames rushed toward him; Paula, several rows ahead, trapped in a mass of twisted metal. If an unexpected business trip hadn't put him on the daily commuter flight the same day that Paula was leaving to go home, what might have happened? Would someone have pulled her from the jammed seat to safety?

"Is something wrong?" She pulled her sweatshirt sleeves down, frowning. "You don't mind that I'm here, do you?"

"Of course not. I'm just surprised." He tried for a coolness he didn't feel. "It didn't bother you, flying back into Bedford Creek again?"

"No." She shook her head, then smiled ruefully.

"I suppose it might have, if I'd tried to do it. I drove up from Baltimore."

Her admission of vulnerability startled him. The Paula he remembered had been proud of her self-reliance and determined not to accept help from anyone. Even after the accident, when he'd awakened in the hospital and learned her family had taken her home to Baltimore for medical care, his offer of financial help had been quickly refused.

"Driving instead of flying sounds reasonable to me," he said. "I don't enjoy getting on a plane now, either."

His own admission shocked him even more. Alexander Caine didn't admit weakness, not to anyone. His father had trained that out of him when he was about his own son's age.

"I haven't been on a plane since..." Paula's gaze flickered away from the scar that accented Alex's cheekbone.

His mouth stiffened, and he read the reaction he should have gotten used to by now. "The plane crash," he finished for her, his tone dry. "You can say the words, you know." He didn't need or want her pity.

"The drive up wasn't bad—just long." She seemed determined to ignore his reference to the crash. She stared at the rows of shelves with their seldom-used dishes as if she really didn't see them. Then her gaze shifted to him. "As I said, I'm on vacation, so I was free to come when Aunt Maida needed me.'' Her expression turned challenging. ''You have noticed she's in pain lately, haven't you?''

He stiffened at the implication of neglect in her pointed question. Of course he felt responsible for the woman who'd cared for his family all these years. But it wasn't Paula Hansen's place to question him.

''I've asked her repeatedly about her health,'' he said. ''She keeps insisting she's fine.''

She lifted her eyebrows, her gaze turning skeptical. Paula's face had always shown her emotions so clearly. A picture flashed into his mind of her lips close to his, her eyes soft.

No. He pushed the errant thought away. *Don't go there.*

''Aunt Maida always insists she's fine. But you must have noticed something.''

''She's been tired and limping more lately.'' He reached behind him for the door, hoping he didn't sound defensive. He was wasting time in this futile discussion—time he didn't have to spare. ''I told her to take it easy this afternoon. She does too much.'' He glanced at the pans scattered on the worn linoleum. ''Instead, she seems to have enlisted you as assistant housekeeper.''

Her chin came up at that, as if it were an insult. ''I'm glad to help my aunt.''

The last time she'd been here, it had been for her brief job as Jason's nanny. Alex tried again to ignore the flood of memories of that time: the laughter and warmth she'd brought to this house, her face turned toward his in the moonlight, the moment he'd forgotten himself and kissed her—

Enough. He'd gotten through the remainder of her stay in Bedford Creek by pretending that kiss had never happened. Paula was probably as eager as he was to avoid the subject.

"I've already told Maida to rest more," he said. "She won't listen."

"It isn't just rest she needs." She stared at him, a question in her green eyes. "You really don't know, do you?"

"Know what?" He couldn't erase the irritation from his tone. "What are you driving at, Paula? I don't have time for guessing games."

Her eyes flashed. "She can't put it off any longer. Aunt Maida has to have hip replacement surgery."

Surgery. The implications staggered him. Maida, the rock on which his home life depended, needed surgery. He fought past a wave of guilt that he hadn't guessed what was going on.

"No, I didn't know." He returned Paula's frown. "I wish Maida *had* told me, but if she didn't want to, that was her right."

"She didn't tell you because she didn't want you to worry."

Paula clearly didn't consider protecting him from worry a priority. Antagonism battled the attraction he felt just looking at her. Maybe it was a good thing she annoyed him so much. It reminded him not to let that attraction get out of control, as it had once before.

"That's ridiculous," he said shortly. "If she needs the operation now, she has to have it. There's no question of that."

Even as he frowned at Paula, his mind raced from one responsibility to another—his son, the factory, the business deal that might save them. His stomach clenched at the thought of the Swiss firm's representative, due to visit any day now. He'd expect to be entertained in Alex's home. How could Alex swing that without Maida's calm, efficient management?

"My aunt knows this is a bad time for you. That's probably why she hasn't told you."

He sensed Paula's disapproval, although whether it was directed at him or her aunt, he didn't know. "I'll manage," he said curtly. "I'll have to find someone to fill in for her, that's all."

He knew when he said it how futile a hope that was. An isolated mountain village didn't boast an army of trained domestics ready for hiring. He'd be lucky to find anyone at all in the middle of the tourist season.

"It won't be easy to hire someone, will it?" She seemed to read his thoughts.

"No. I'm afraid Maida has spoiled us." He should have known things couldn't run so smoothly forever.

"Aunt Maida thinks she has a solution, if you'll go along with it."

He realized Paula was carefully not looking at him, and that fact sent up a red flag of warning. "What is it?"

Paula took a deep breath and fixed him with a look that was half embarrassed, half defiant. "She wants you to hire me as her replacement."

For a long moment he could only stare at her. Paula—back in his house, cooking his meals, looking after his son. Given what had happened between them the last time she worked for him, he couldn't believe she'd be willing to try it again.

One thing he could believe, though. Having Paula Hansen in his house again wouldn't just be embarrassing. Having her there, seeing her every day, no matter how desperately he needed help— that would be downright insane.

The expression on Alex's lean, aristocratic face showed Paula only too well exactly what he thought of her aunt's idea. Why on earth hadn't Aunt Maida told him before Paula arrived? Maida knew this situation would be difficult. She'd said she'd prepare the way. Instead, she'd brought Paula here without saying a word to Alex about it.

Of course, Aunt Maida couldn't have known her niece would go weak-kneed at the sight of Alex Caine.

"I see." Alex's tone was coolly noncommittal, and the polite, well-bred mask he habitually wore slid into place.

It was too late. Naturally he wouldn't come right out and tell her he didn't want her in his house again. But she'd seen his swift, unguarded reaction. Her heart sank. She should have known he wouldn't agree to this.

"Where is Maida? We need to talk about this."

"She's not here." She took a deep breath and prepared for an explosion. *Oh, Aunt Maida. Why didn't you tell him?* "She's already checked into the hospital in Henderson."

He started to speak, then clamped his mouth closed. Maybe he was counting to ten. She could only hope it worked.

"She's scheduled for surgery tomorrow." She might as well get it all out. If he intended to explode, he'd just have to do it once. "I guess she thought I could help out here, at least until you make a decision about replacing her."

"You said she didn't want to worry me. Did she

think this wasn't worrying—going to the hospital and leaving you to break the news?''

The fine lines around Alex's dark eyes seemed to deepen. She longed to smooth them away with her fingertips. The urge, so strong her skin tingled, shocked her. She couldn't think that, couldn't feel it.

She didn't have a good answer to his question. ''I thought she planned to tell you. When we talked on the phone last week, she said she would.''

Maida had sounded so desperate. *''I need you, Paula. Jason needs you. That child is hurting, and you might be the only one who can help him.''* Maida must not have wanted to risk telling Alex, and his finding some other solution to her absence. She could only pray Maida was right.

''Why didn't you tell me, then?''

Alex's intense, dark stare seemed to pierce right through her, finding the vulnerabilities she longed to hide. She took a deep breath, trying to quell jittery nerves. She'd known it would be difficult to come back here. She just hadn't anticipated *how* difficult. If Aunt Maida knew how hard this was for her—

No, she couldn't let Maida know that. She'd agreed to do this thing, and she had to do it.

''I am telling you. I mean, now you know, don't you?'' She clenched her hands together, hoping he didn't realize how much of her attitude was bravado. "Look, all I know is that she said she'd tell you. I thought it was all arranged. That's why I'm here—" she gestured toward the scattered pots "—trying to fix dinner for you and Jason."

Alex looked if it was the worst idea he'd ever heard. If he sent her packing, she'd never have a chance to make up for the mistakes she'd made the last time she was here.

"I can cook, you know," she assured him. "I learned from the best." Maida had insisted on giving her cooking lessons every time Paula came to visit.

"Of course you're going to get an education and have a profession," Maida would say. *"But it never does any harm to know how to cook."*

He looked at her skeptically, and her doubts rose. Why was this so difficult?

Lord, if this really is the right thing to do, please let me know it.

"Dinner tonight isn't important." His voice was clipped. "I'll take Jason out for a hamburger—he always welcomes that. As for the rest of it, I'll make a decision later. You can go to the hospital to see Maida. Tell her I'll be there tomorrow."

She nodded, trying not to react to his tone. As heir to the Caine family fortune, he'd probably been born with the commanding manner that assumed compliance with his orders. The quality never failed to irritate Paula, but Alex had a right to make his own decisions about his staff. And if she did work for him, he'd also have a perfect right to give her orders and expect obedience.

Seeming to consider the matter settled, Alex turned toward the front of the house.

She wanted to let him go, because his disturbing presence upset her equilibrium and made her silly heart flutter. But she couldn't. There was too much yet to be settled. She had to convince him that she was the right person for this job.

She caught up with him at the swinging door marking the boundary between the family's part of the mansion and the servants' section.

"Alex—" She put her hand on his arm to stop him, and was instantly sorry. Through the silky broadcloth of his shirt, his skin warmed to her touch. He wore the dress shirt and tie that was part of his usual attire, but the sleeves were turned back at the wrists, exposing a gold watchband that gleamed against his skin.

She pulled her gaze from his hands, fighting for balance, and focused on his face, instead. It didn't help. He bore lines he hadn't two years ago, and the narrow scar that crossed his cheekbone added an attractively dangerous look to his even, classic features.

She snatched her hand away. "I mean, Mr. Caine." She felt her cheeks flushing. Observing the proprieties might help keep things businesslike between them. It might prevent a recurrence of what happened two years ago.

He stopped, looking down at her, his dark eyes unreadable beneath winged brows. Then he shook his head.

"You've been calling me Alex since the first time you came here. You were only about Jason's age."

She nodded, deflected by memories of the past. At least Alex seemed able to put his antagonism aside for the moment and remember a more peaceful time. That had to be a good sign.

"I was eight. And homesick as could be. You showed me where the children's books were in the library and told me to help myself."

She'd been awestruck when Alex Caine, only child of the town's richest man and the prince in the Caine castle, had made the effort to be kind to her. She'd felt like Cinderella when he'd led her into the elegant room lined with books and shown her the window seat next to the fireplace where she could curl up and read. Not that she'd ever done it when there was a chance his formidable father might find her.

"So we're old friends." The smile that came too rarely lit his lean face, causing an uncomfortable flutter somewhere in the vicinity of her heart. "Alex will do."

"Alex," she repeated, trying not to linger on his

name. "You know how stubborn Aunt Maida can be. I'm sure she was just doing what she thought would cause the least trouble. If she could have delayed the surgery, she would have, but the doctor insisted."

She wanted to say the words that would convince him to let her stay, but she couldn't find them. Instead, she swung back to her worries about Maida.

"She told me Dr. Overton retired. Someone else took over his practice."

"You can have confidence in Brett Elliot," he said promptly, apparently reading her concern. "He's an excellent doctor, and I'm sure he's recommended the best surgeon." A hint of a smile touched his lips again. "And I'm not saying that because Brett's an old friend."

She suddenly saw herself as a child, peering from the housekeeper's cottage toward the swimming pool. A teenage Alex entertained two other boys: Mitch Donovan and Brett Elliot, his closest friends.

"Aunt Maida seems to trust him. That's the important thing."

He nodded, hand on the door. She could sense the impatience in him, as if he wanted to be elsewhere, as if only his deeply ingrained politeness kept him standing there.

She probably should let this go, but she couldn't. She took a breath. "I know Aunt Maida's suggestion has put you on the spot. But it really would ease her mind if she knew I was staying.''

She knew instantly she'd pressed too hard. He seemed to withdraw, putting distance between them even though he hadn't moved. His face set in bleak lines.

Alex had never looked that way when she was growing up. He'd always been surrounded by a golden aura nothing could diminish. But that had been before his wife left, before he'd spent too many weeks in that hospital himself.

"Let's get the immediate situation taken care of first," he said. "You settle Maida at the hospital. If she needs anything, she just has to ask."

"I know that. I'm sure Maida does, too." She tried to deny a wave of resentment that he could so easily grant any wish of her aunt's, while she couldn't.

He clasped her hand, sending a surge of warmth along her skin and stealing her breath. Then he dropped it as abruptly as if he'd felt that heat.

"Maida will be glad to have you with her for the operation. I know how much she enjoyed it when you worked here."

He almost seemed to stumble over the words, as if he found this situation as awkward as she did. It surprised her. Smooth, sophisticated Alex had never been at a loss for the right phrase. That ability was something else the upper crust seemed to be born with.

All the things she didn't want to say about the time she worked in the Caine mansion skittered through her mind. Still, it wouldn't hurt to remind him that his son already knew her. "I appreciated the chance to take care of Jason. How is he?"

"Fine." His face seemed to stiffen again. "Looking forward to summer vacation after the rigors of second grade."

She had the sense of something suppressed, something he didn't want to say about his son, and thought again of Aunt Maida's worries about the boy.

"He used to be such a happy child. But his mother went away, and then Alex was in the accident and in the hospital all those weeks. Jason's changed. He's all curled up inside himself, and I don't know how to help him."

"I'm looking forward to seeing him." She tried to keep the words casual. "Does he really want a fast-food burger, or did you just make that up?"

"Believe it or not, he does. Maida and I try to educate his palate, but he's very much a seven-year-old in his tastes." The skin at the corners of his eyes crinkled. "I think you gave him his first trip to get fast food when you took care of him, didn't you?"

"I'm afraid so." She remembered it as if it were

yesterday. Jason's excitement at ordering from the counter, the awed look on his face as he sat across from her in the booth. The feelings that welled up at how much he resembled his father. That emotion struck her again, as strong as if someone had hit her.

Lord, what's happening to me? I thought I was over this.

Alex's dark, intent gaze penetrated the barrier she'd so carefully erected to shield her errant emotions. "What is it? What's wrong?"

"Nothing." She looked up and summoned a smile that felt tight on her lips. "Everything's okay."

She'd like to convince him. She'd like to convince herself. Alex couldn't know that, thanks to the accident, for nearly two years she hadn't been able to remember the crash or the months that had preceded it.

He didn't know that the memories of the time she'd spent in this house had fallen out of the hidden recesses of her mind a week ago, as fresh and as emotional as if they'd happened yesterday.

And prominent among them was the fact that the last time she was here, she'd fallen in love with Alex Caine.

Chapter Two

"Dad, is Maida going to come back?"

The forlorn note in his son's voice touched Alex's heart. What did Jason fear? That Maida had gone away and would never come back, like his mother?

Careful, careful. "What makes you think she won't come back?"

Alex glanced across the front seat of the car. Jason, who'd seemed happy enough at the restaurant, now sat clutching the plastic action figure that had come with his meal.

He frowned down at the figure, then looked up, his small face tightening into the mask that frustrated Alex as much as it did Jason's teachers.

Where has he gone, Lord? Where is the sunny little boy Jason used to be?

He felt almost embarrassed at the involuntary prayer, and his hands tightened on the wheel with determination. He was all Jason had, and he wouldn't let him down.

His son shouldn't have to worry, about Maida or anything else. Naturally he'd had to tell Jason something to explain Maida's absence, but he'd said as little as possible.

"She's just tired," he said now, trying to sound cheerful. "She needs to rest more. It's nothing you have to be concerned about. She'll be back before you know it, and everything will be fine."

They passed twin stone pillars and swung into the driveway. Paula, still wearing the jeans and sweatshirt that seemed to be her uniform, was bending over the trunk of a disreputable old car in his garage. She looked up at their approach, and he pulled into the bay next to her. When he got out, she was already explaining.

"I hope this is okay. Aunt Maida said you wouldn't mind if I parked my car here." She glanced down the row of empty bays, a question in her eyes.

"No problem. I got rid of the other cars after my father died."

Nobody needed five cars. His father had insisted on trying to relive the old days, when a full-time chauffeur had taken loving care of a fleet of vehicles, a full-time gardener tended the roses, and

Maida supervised a staff of three indoors. Now they made do with a cleaning company and a lawn service, with Maida watching Jason when he wasn't in school.

He waited for Paula to make some comment, but her attention was fixed on the small figure coming around the car.

"Jason, hi. It's good to see you again."

Jason nodded warily, always seeming on guard with strangers. Not that Paula was exactly a stranger, but at his age, two years was a long time.

"Hey, you got the green Raider." She touched the action figure Jason held. "Good going. He's the best, isn't he?"

His son's protective stance relaxed a little. "One of the guys in my class says the orange one's better, but I like the green one. He can do cool stuff."

"He sure can. Did you see the story where he rescued the princess?"

"Yeah. And when he set all the horses free. That was neat." Jason's face grew animated as he talked about the latest adventure of his action hero.

How had Paula gotten past his son's defenses so quickly? Alex felt something that might have been envy, then dismissed it. She was a teacher—she should be good with children.

Paula pulled a duffel bag from the trunk, and Alex reached out to take it from her. It was heavier than it looked, and for a moment their hands entangled.

"Rocks?" he enquired, lifting an eyebrow.

"Books." She made an abortive movement, as if to take the bag back, then seemed to think better of it. "I never go anywhere without them."

He glanced into the car's trunk. One cardboard carton overflowed with construction paper, and a plastic Halloween pumpkin poked improbably from another. "It looks as if you've brought everything you own."

He meant the comment lightly, but a shadow crossed her face. It told him more clearly than words that how long she stayed depended on him. She shrugged, turning to pull out another bag.

"Most of this stuff is from my classroom. I loaded it up the last day and didn't take the time to unload before I left to come here."

"I'll carry that one." Jason reached for the small bag.

"Thanks, Jason." She smiled, surrendering it to him, then hefted a box out and slammed the trunk. "I think that's it." She glanced at Alex. "If you're sure it's okay for me to leave the car here?"

"It's fine," he said firmly. He'd rather see that poor excuse for a car hidden behind garage doors than parked in his drive. Lifting the duffel bag, he led the way around down the walk toward the rear of the house.

The setting sun turned the swimming pool's surface to gold as they neared the flagstone patio. He hadn't done the water exercises for his injured leg today, and it took an effort to walk evenly carrying the heavy bag. He'd already seen Paula's expression at the scar on his face. He didn't want to see more pity if she caught him limping.

What did she really think about this idea of Maida's? Had it made her remember what happened between them the last time she was here?

One kiss, that was all. It was ridiculous to worry about the effect of one kiss. Of course he shouldn't have done it. She'd been working in his house, and that alone made her out of bounds to him.

Even if that hadn't been the case, he'd learned something when his wife's death, so soon after she'd left him, had made patching up their failing marriage impossible. Even if Karin had survived, even if she'd come back to the small-town life she detested, he'd known then that finding the love of a lifetime was an illusion. Reality was raising his son properly and maintaining the business this whole town relied on. He didn't intend to chase any more romantic rainbows.

So what was he doing watching Paula's smooth, easy stride, eyeing the swing of blond hair against her shoulder when she looked down to smile at Jason? He should have better sense.

She paused at the pool, bending to dip her fingers

in the water. "Nice. I'll bet you're in the pool all the time, now that school's out."

Jason shrugged. "Mostly my dad uses it. To make his leg better."

Alex braced himself for the look of pity, but she just nodded.

"Good idea."

"If you'd like to use the pool while you're here, please do." He disliked the stilted tone of his voice. Paula's presence had thrown him off balance. She was part of an embarrassing incident in his past, and she was also a reminder of the plane crash.

But she'd probably long since forgotten about that kiss. As for the accident, that was something every survivor had to deal with in his own way.

"Thanks." She stood. "I don't know if I'll be here that long."

Her words challenged him, but he wouldn't be drawn in. He'd ignore that particular problem for the moment. Jason had gotten several strides ahead, leaving them side by side. As they headed for the housekeeper's cottage, Alex lowered his voice. "How did Maida seem when you visited her? I hope she's not too worried about the surgery. Or about not having told me. She needs to concentrate on getting well, rather than worrying about us."

She hesitated, frown lines creasing her forehead. "She seems to trust the doctor to put things right. We didn't talk long."

"That sounds a bit evasive."

She shot him an annoyed look. "Don't you think it would be more polite not to say so?"

He'd forgotten that directness of hers. It made him smile—when it wasn't irritating him. "I'm worried about Maida, too. Remember?"

"Are you?"

"Yes." All right, now he was annoyed. Maybe that was a safer way to feel with Paula, anyway. "Believe it or not, you're not the only one who cares about her."

Her clear green eyes seemed to weigh his sincerity. Then she nodded with a kind of cautious acceptance. "The surgeon says she should come through the operation with flying colors, and then Brett will supervise her rehabilitation. That'll take time, and he wouldn't guess how long until she can come home."

He glanced at his son. "I haven't mentioned the surgery to Jason. I just said Maida needed a rest. The less he knows, the better."

She frowned as if disagreeing, but didn't argue. She moved toward his son. "Just put that on the porch, Jason. I'll take it in later."

She dropped her bags and sat down on the step, then patted the spot next to her. "Have a seat and tell me what's been going on. I haven't seen you for a long time."

Jason sat cautiously, seeming ready to dart away at a moment's notice.

Had Alex been that shy when he was Jason's age? He thought not, but then his father had always insisted on the social graces, no matter what he actually felt. Maybe, if his mother had lived, things would have been different. He stood stiffly, not comfortable with sitting down next to them, not willing to walk away, either.

"Bet you're glad school's out for the summer," Paula said. "I know my kids were."

Jason glanced up at her. "You have kids?"

"My students," she corrected herself. "I teach kindergarten. My school finished up yesterday, and everyone celebrated. Did you have a party the last day?"

Jason nodded. "We played games. And Maida made cupcakes for me to take."

Alex hadn't known that, but, of course, it was the sort of thing Maida would do. He shifted uncomfortably, trying to ease the pain in his leg. With the crucial business deal pending, he'd had trouble keeping up with anything else lately, including second-grade parties. He should go in and get back to work, but still he lingered, watching Paula with his son.

"I'll bet the kids liked those," she said. "Maida makes the best cupcakes."

Jason nodded, glancing down at the step he was

scuffing with the toe of his shoe. Then he looked up at Paula. "Did you come here to teach me?"

"Teach you?" she echoed. "Why would I do that? School's out for the summer."

Jason shrugged, not looking at either of them. "My dad thinks I should do better in school."

Shock took Alex's breath away for a moment. Then he found his voice. "Jason, I don't think that at all. And it's not something we should talk about to Paula, anyway."

Paula ignored him, all her attention focused on Jason. Her hand rested lightly on his son's shoulder. "Hey, second grade is tough for lots of people. I remember how hard it was when I had to start writing instead of printing. My teacher said my cursive looked like chicken scratches."

"Honest?" Jason darted a glance at her.

"Honest." She smiled at him. "You can ask Aunt Maida if you don't believe me. She probably remembers when I used to try to write letters to her. Sometimes she'd call me to find out what I'd said."

She'd managed to wipe the tension from Jason's face with a few words. Alex didn't know whether to be pleased or jealous that she'd formed such instant rapport with his son. Paula seemed to have a talent for inspiring mixed feelings in him.

Her blond hair swung across her cheek as she leaned toward Jason, saying something. The impulse to reach out and brush it back was so strong that his hand actually started to move before common sense took over.

Mixed feelings, indeed. The predominant feeling he had toward Paula Hansen wasn't mixed at all. It was one he'd better ignore, for both their sakes.

Paula stood on the tiny porch of the housekeeper's cottage the next morning, looking across the expansive grounds that glistened from last night's shower. The sun, having made it over the steep mountains surrounding Bedford Creek, slanted toward the birch tree at the end of the pool, turning its wet leaves to silver. The only sound that pierced the stillness was the persistent call of a bobwhite.

The stillness had made this secluded village seem like a haven to her when she was a child. She'd arrived in the Pennsylvania mountains from Baltimore, leaving behind the crowded row house echoing with the noise her brothers made. Four brothers—all of them older, all of them thinking they had the right to boss her around. Her childhood had sometimes seemed like one long battle—for privacy, for space, for the freedom to be who she was.

Here she'd stepped into a different world—one with nature on the doorstep, one filled with order and quiet. She couldn't possibly imagine the Caine mansion putting up with a loud game of keep-away in its center hall. It would have ejected the intruders forcibly.

Paula glanced toward the back of the mansion, wondering how much Alex had changed it since his father's death. The room on the end was the solarium. She remembered it filled with plants, but Alex had apparently converted it to a workout room. She could see the equipment through the floor-to-ceiling windows.

Next came the kitchen, with its smaller windows overlooking the pool. She should be there right now, fixing breakfast for Alex and Jason, but Alex had made it very clear he didn't want that.

Aunt Maida wasn't going to be happy. The last thing she'd said the night before had been to fix breakfast. Paula's protests—that Alex had told her not to, that Alex hadn't agreed to let her stay yet— had fallen on deaf ears.

Maida's stubborn streak was legendary in the Hansen family. Paula's father was the same, and any battle between Maida and him was a clash of wills. She vividly remembered the war over Maida's determination that Paula go to college. If not for Maida, Paula might have given up, accepting her father's dictum that girls got marriage certificates, not degrees. Her dream of a profession might have remained a dream.

But Maida wouldn't allow that. She'd pushed, encouraged, demanded. Paula had worked two jobs for most of the four years of college, but she'd made it through, thanks to Aunt Maida.

She leaned against the porch rail, watching a pair of wrens twittering in the thick yew hedge that stretched from the housekeeper's cottage toward the garage. If only she could find a way to help her aunt, to help Jason, without being a servant in Alex Caine's house.

She and Jason had played on the flagstone patio when she was his nanny. They'd sat in the gazebo with a storybook, and he'd leaned against her confidently, his small head burrowed against her arm. She remembered, so well, the vulnerable curve of his neck, the little-boy smell of him. He'd look up at her, his dark eyes so like his father's, sure he could trust her, sure she'd be there for him. And then she'd gone away.

What am I supposed to do, Lord? If Alex said no, would she be upset or would she be relieved? Only the guilt she felt over Jason kept her from running in the opposite direction rather than face Alex Caine every day and remember how he'd kissed her and then turned away, embarrassed.

Infatuation, she told herself sternly. It was infatuation, nothing more. She would stop imagining it was love.

She remembered, only too clearly, standing in the moonlight looking up at him, her feelings surely written on her face. Then recognition swept over her. Alex regretted that kiss. He probably thought she'd invited it. Humiliation flooded her, as harsh and scalding as acid.

She'd mumbled some excuse and run back to Aunt Maida's cottage. And a few days later, when she'd realized the feelings weren't going to fade, she'd made another excuse and left her job several weeks earlier than she'd intended, prepared to scurry back to Baltimore.

The flow of memories slowed, sputtering to a painful halt. Her last clear recollection was of Alex lifting her suitcase into the limo next to his own, saying he had to take the commuter flight out that day, too. Then—nothing. She'd eventually regained the rest of her memories, but the actual take-off and crash remained hidden, perhaps gone forever.

When she'd recovered enough to ask questions, her parents had simply said she'd been on her way home from her summer job. If she'd remembered then, would she have done anything differently? She wasn't sure. The failure had lain hidden in her mind.

Now, according to Aunt Maida, anyway, God was giving her a chance to make up for whatever mistakes she'd made then. Unlike most of the people Paula knew, Aunt Maida never hesitated to bring God into every decision.

Whether Maida was right about God's will, Paula didn't know. But her aunt was right about one

thing—Jason had changed. Paula pictured his wary
expression, the way he hunched his shoulders. The
happy child he'd been once had vanished.

Of course, he was old enough now to understand
a little more about his mother's leaving. That trau-
matic event, followed so soon by the plane crash
that injured his father, was enough to cause problems for any child. And he must know that his
mother wouldn't be coming back. Maida had told
her the details that hadn't appeared in Karin's brief
obituary—the wild party, the drunken driver. Paula
frowned, thinking of students who'd struggled with
similar losses.

A flicker of movement beyond the yew hedge
caught her eye. Between the glossy dark leaves, she
glimpsed a bright yellow shirt. She'd thought Jason
was at breakfast with his father. What was he doing?

She rounded the corner of the cottage and spotted
the child. The greeting she'd been about to call out
died on her lips. All her teacher instincts went on
alert. She might not know Jason well any longer,
but she knew what a kid up to something looked
like. Jason bent over something on the ground, his
body shielding it from her view.

She moved quietly across the grass. "Jason?
What's up?"

He jerked around at her voice, dropping the object he held. The crumpled paper lit with a sudden spark, a flame shooting up.

She winced back, heart pounding, stomach contracting. *Run!* a voice screamed in her head. *Run!*

She took a breath, then another. She didn't need to run. Nothing would hurt her. *It's all right.* She repeated the comforting words over in her mind. It was all right.

Except that it wasn't. Quite aside from the terror of fire that had plagued her since the accident, what was Jason doing playing with matches? Another thought jolted her. Was this connected with his father's narrow escape from a fiery death?

Carefully she stepped on the spark that remained, grinding it into the still-wet grass. The scent of burning lingered in the air, sickening her.

She looked at Jason, and he took a quick step back. "Where'd you get the matches, Jason?"

His lower lip came out. "I don't know what you're talking about. I don't have any matches."

"Sure you do." She held out her hand. "Give them to me."

Maybe it was the calm, authoritative "teacher" voice. Jason dug into his jeans' pocket, pulled out the matchbook and dropped it into her hand.

She closed her fingers firmly around it. She wouldn't let them tremble. "Where did you get this?"

For a moment she thought he wouldn't answer.

He glared at her, dark eyes defiant. Then he shrugged. "My dad's desk. Are you gonna tell him?"

"I think someone should, don't you?" It would hardly be surprising if Jason's unresolved feelings about his father's accident had led to a fascination with fire. Not surprising, but dangerous.

"No!" His anger flared so suddenly that it caught her by surprise. His small fists clenched. "Leave me alone."

"Jason..." She reached toward him, impelled by the need to comfort him, but he dodged away from her.

"Go away!" He nearly shouted the words. "Just go away!" He turned and ran toward the house.

She discovered she was shaking and wrapped her arms around herself. Jason had made his feelings clear. His was definitely a vote for her to leave.

Alex put the weights back on their rack and stretched, gently flexing his injured knee. Brett Elliot, one of his oldest friends as well as his doctor, would personally supervise his workouts if he thought Alex was skipping them. And Brett was right; Alex had to admit it. The exercise therapy had brought him miles from where he'd been after the accident.

He toweled off, then picked up his juice bottle and stepped through the French doors to the flagstones surrounding the pool. The water looked tempting with the hot June sunshine bouncing from its surface, but he had another goal in mind at the moment. Jason was off on some game of his own. It was time Alex talked to Paula. He had to find some graceful way to get them both out of this difficult situation, in spite of the fact that he hadn't yet found someone else to replace Maida.

His timing seemed perfect. Paula was coming around the pool toward the house, dressed a bit formally for her. Instead of her usual jeans, she wore neat tan slacks and a bright coral top—probably a concession for a trip to the hospital. She briefly checked her swift stride when she saw him, and then she came toward him.

"Good morning." He tossed the towel over his shoulder and set his juice bottle on the patio table. *Business,* he reminded himself. "I hoped I'd have a chance to see you this morning."

Paula rubbed her arms, as if she were cold in spite of the June sunshine. "Aren't you going to the factory today?"

"Not until later," he said. "I'll work at home for a while, then stop by the hospital to see how Maida's doing." He hesitated, looking for words, but since Paula was so direct herself, she should appreciate the same from him. "We should get a few things settled."

For just an instant Paula's eyes were puzzled, as

if she'd been thinking about something else entirely. Then she gave him a wary look and took a step back.

"I have to leave for the hospital." She glanced at her watch. "I want to be there when Aunt Maida wakes up from the operation."

"This will take just a few minutes. We've got to discuss this idea of Maida's." He knew he sounded inflexible, but he didn't want to put this off. The longer he waited, the more difficult it would be.

He pulled out a deck chair for her. Looking reluctant, she sat down. He settled in the seat next to her and instantly regretted his choice. They were facing the gazebo at the end of the pool. They shouldn't be having this conversation in view of the spot where he'd kissed her.

But it was too late now, and maybe it was just as well. That embarrassing episode should make her as reluctant as he was to pursue Maida's scheme. He'd give her an easy way out of this dilemma, that was all. And she'd be ready to leave.

Paula tugged at the sleeves of her knit top. Apparently she did that whenever she was nervous, as if she were protecting herself. He tried not to notice how the coral sweater brought out the warm, peachy color in her cheeks, or how the fine gold chain she wore glinted against her skin.

Stick to business, he ordered himself. That was a good way to think of it. This was just like any business negotiation, and they both needed to go away from it feeling they'd gained something.

"Be honest with me, Paula. You don't really want to work here this summer, do you?"

She glanced up at him, a startled expression in her eyes. "What makes you say that?"

To his surprise, he couldn't quite get the real reason out. *Because the last time you were here, I kissed you and created an awkward situation for both of us. Because in spite of that, I still find you too attractive for my own peace of mind.*

No, he didn't want to say any of that. He tried a different tack.

"You probably had a teaching job of some sort lined up for the summer, didn't you?"

She shook her head, a rueful smile touching her lips. "There's not much teaching available in the summer. I was signed up with a temp agency for office work."

"Office work?" He couldn't stop the surprise in his voice, and realized instantly how condescending it sounded. "Why? I mean, couldn't you find anything else?"

Her expression suggested he didn't have a clue as to how the real world worked. "Kindergarten teachers aren't exactly on corporate headhunters' wish lists, you know."

"But aren't there courses you want to take in the summer?" He didn't know why the thought of

Paula taking temporary work to make ends meet bothered him so much. His reaction was totally irrational.

"I can't afford to take classes." She said it slowly and distinctly, as if they spoke different languages. "I have college loans to pay off."

Belatedly he reminded himself he was supposed to be dissuading her from working for him. "Even so, I can't imagine that you'd want to come here to cook and take care of Jason, instead."

He saw immediately that he'd said the wrong thing. In fact, he'd probably said a lot of wrong things. Paula had that effect on him.

She stiffened, and anger flared in her face. "Cooking is honest work. There's nothing to be ashamed of in what my aunt does," she snapped, and she gripped the arms of the deck chair as if about to launch herself out of it.

"No, of course not." He seemed to be going even farther in the wrong direction. "I didn't mean to imply that."

She stood, anger coming off her in waves. "I really have to leave for the hospital now, Alex. I've told my aunt I'm willing to fill in for her here as long as necessary, but, of course, you may have other plans. Either way, it's up to you."

She spun on her heel before he could find words to stop her. He watched her stalk toward the garage, head high.

Great. That was certainly the clumsiest negotiation he'd ever attempted. If he did that poorly in the business deal, the plant would be closed within a month.

Paula had thrown the decision right back into his lap, and she'd certainly made her position clear. If he didn't want her here, he'd have to be the one to say it. Unfortunately, where Paula was concerned, he really wasn't sure what he wanted.

Chapter Three

Alex hadn't hired her, and maybe he wouldn't. But she couldn't just let things go. Paula pulled into the garage late that afternoon, aware of how pitiful her junker looked in the cavernous building. Aunt Maida was still groggy from the successful surgery, but she'd soon be well enough to demand a report. Paula had to be able to reassure her.

She walked quickly to the back door of the mansion. A small bicycle leaned against the laundry room door, reminding her of Jason and the matches. She should have told Alex, but their conversation had veered off in another direction entirely, and she hadn't found the words. Maybe she still hadn't.

Even the geranium on the kitchen window sill seemed to droop in Maida's absence. Breakfast dishes, stacked in the sink, made it clear that when

Alex said he'd fix breakfast for himself and Jason, he hadn't considered cleaning up. She turned the water on. It wasn't her job. Alex hadn't hired her. But Maida's kitchen had always been spotless, and she couldn't leave it this way.

This was for Maida, she told herself, plunging her hands into hot, sudsy water. Not for Alex.

She'd been angry at Alex's implications about the housekeeper position, but she'd been just as guilty of thinking Maida's job less important than her own. Now it was the job she needed and wanted to fill—if only she could erase the memory of Alex's kiss.

Enough. She concentrated on rubbing each piece of the sterling flatware. She'd come here to make up for the past by helping Jason through this difficult time. That was all.

She heard the door swing behind her and turned. Jason stood staring at her. For a moment he didn't move. Then he came toward her slowly. He stopped a few feet away.

"I came to say I'm sorry."

"Are you, Jason?" Was it regret or good manners that brought him here? Maybe it didn't really matter. At least he was talking. That was better than silence.

"I shouldn't have yelled at you." A quiver of apprehension crossed his face. "Did you tell my dad?"

"No." She pulled out a chair at the pine kitchen table. "I think Maida has some lemonade in the refrigerator. Want a glass?"

He nodded a little stiffly. "That would be nice."

He was like his father, in manner as well as in looks, she thought as she poured two glasses of lemonade. Same dark hair and eyes, same well-defined bone structure, same strict courtesy.

He didn't have the stiff upper lip to his father's degree of perfection, though. He watched her apprehensively as she sat down across from him.

"I don't want to tell him." The words surprised her. Surely she should—but if she did, she'd never get beyond the barrier Jason seemed to have erected against the world. "I think *you* should, though. It's pretty serious stuff. You could have gotten hurt."

"I won't do it again." Dark eyes pleaded with her. "Promise you won't say anything. I won't do it again, honest."

She studied his expression. Even at seven or eight, a lot of kids had figured out how to tell adults what they wanted to hear, instead of the truth. But Jason seemed genuinely dismayed at the result of his actions.

She took a deep breath. *Let me make the right decision. Please.*

"Okay, Jason. If you promise you won't do it again, I promise I won't tell."

His relieved smile was the first one she'd seen

from him. *Like his father,* she thought again. A smile that rare made you want to forgive anything, just to see it.

Jason didn't seem to have inherited any qualities from his mother. Did he miss her and wonder why she'd disappeared? Maybe by now he'd made peace with his loss.

She watched as he gulped the lemonade. Guilt seemed to have made him thirsty. Finally he set the glass down, looking at it, not at her.

"Is Maida really going to come back?"

The question startled her. "Sure she is. Why do you think she wouldn't?"

"I heard Daddy talking." He fixed her with an intent gaze. "He told me she just needed to rest a while, but I heard him tell somebody on the phone that she was in the hospital. Is she going to stay there?"

Never lie to a child; that was one of her bedrock beliefs as a teacher. If something was going to hurt, going to be unpleasant, a child had the same right as an adult to prepare for it.

"Only for a little while," she said carefully, remembering Alex's determination to shield his son. "She had to go into the hospital to have her hip fixed."

His face clouded. "I don't want her to stay there. Can't Dr. Brett just give her some medicine?"

The bereft tone touched her. "I know you don't

want her to be away, but medicine won't fix what's wrong. She had to have an operation, and they gave her a brand-new joint. Now she has to stay at the hospital and do exercises until she's better.''

"Like my dad does for his leg?"

"Sort of like that." She seemed to see Alex again in the workout clothes he'd worn that morning, and her mouth went dry. "Then when she's well, she'll be able to come back.''

His gaze met hers, and she read a challenge in it. "You didn't come back. Not for a long time.''

It was like a blow to the heart. Jason was talking about when she'd been his nanny. Maybe, underneath the words, he was thinking about his mother, too.

She longed to put her hand over his where it lay on the table, but he was such a prickly child that she was afraid of making him withdraw. She prayed for the right words.

"I want you to listen, Jason, because I'm telling you the truth. Maida loves you. If she could have skipped the operation to stay with you, she would have. She's going to come back, and in the meantime, you'll be okay.''

"Are you going to stay?" His lips trembled. "Are you? I know I said I wanted you to go away, but I didn't mean it. I want you to stay.''

Guilt gripped her throat in a vise so tight she couldn't speak. She'd asked God to show her what to do. Was this His answer, in the voice of a troubled little boy?

She cleared her throat. "I'm not sure, Jason. But I'm going to talk to your daddy about it."

"When?" Urgency filled his voice. "When?"

Somehow, whatever it took, she had to convince Alex to let her stay. She stood. "Right now."

Alex had been trying to concentrate on work for the past half-hour, but all he could think about was how he'd manage the coming weeks. His business, his family, his home were too intertwined to separate.

He didn't have any illusions that it would be easy to replace Maida. First of all, no one *could* really replace her. She was the closest thing to a mother Jason had.

Tension radiated down his spine. Jason had had enough losses in his young life. It was up to his father to protect him from any more.

It was also up to his father to provide for his future. If this deal with Dieter Industries didn't go through, and soon, the Caine company would be on the verge of collapse. Their hand-crafted furniture would go the way of the lumber mills founded by his great-grandfather. Probably not even his private fortune could save it. Several hundred people would be out of work, thanks to Caine Industries's failure.

He didn't have the luxury of time. Dieter was

sending someone over within weeks. Alex had to be ready, or they all lost.

He glanced up at the portrait of his father that hung over the library's tile fireplace. Jonathan Caine stared sternly from the heavy gold frame, as if he mentally weighed and measured everyone he saw and found them wanting. He would no more understand the firm's current crisis than he'd be able to admit that his mistakes had led to it.

His father's stroke and death, coming when he heard the news of the crash, had seemed the knockout blow. But Alex had found out, once he took over, just how badly off the company was. And he'd realized there were still blows to come. He'd spent the past two years trying to solve the company's problems, and he still didn't know if he could succeed.

This was getting him nowhere. Alex walked to the floor-length window and looked down at the town—his town. He knew every inch of its steep narrow streets, folded into the cleft of the mountains. Sometimes he thought he knew every soul in town.

Caines had taken care of Bedford Creek since the first Caine, a railroad baron, had built his mansion on the hill in the decade after the Civil War. Bedford Creek had two economic bases: its scenic beauty and Caine Industries. If the corporation went under, how would the town survive? How would he?

The rap on the door was tentative. Then it came again, stronger this time. He crossed the room with impatient steps and opened the door.

"Paula." That jolt to his solar plexus each time he saw her ought to be getting familiar by now. "I'm sorry, but this isn't a good time."

"This is important."

What was one more disruption to his day? He wasn't getting anything accomplished, anyway. He stepped back, gesturing her in.

"Is something wrong?"

She swung to face him. "Have you made a decision about hiring someone to replace my aunt?"

He motioned to a chair, but she shook her head, planting herself in the center of the oriental carpet and looking at him.

"Not yet," he admitted. "Summer is tourist season in Bedford Creek. Everyone who wants a job is probably already working."

He couldn't deny the fact that Maida had been right about one thing. Paula could be the answer to his problems. But the uncomfortable ending to her previous stay, his own mixed feelings for her, made that impossible. He couldn't seem to get past that.

"You have to have someone Jason can get along with." She hesitated. "I couldn't help thinking that he's changed."

He stiffened. "My son is fine." *Fine,* he repeated silently.

"He seems to believe you're disappointed in his school work."

Her clear, candid gaze bored into him. "He misunderstood," he said shortly. "Jason is very bright." He glared at her, daring her to disagree.

"Yes, of course he is. But that doesn't mean school is easy for him."

"Paula, I don't want to discuss my son with you. Jason is fine. Now, is there anything else?"

She looked at him for what felt like a long moment, and he couldn't tell what was going on behind her usually expressive face. Then her eyes flickered.

"Just one thing. You should hire me to fill in until Maida is well again."

Paula's heart pounded in her ears. She hadn't intended to blurt it out like that. She'd thought she'd lead up to it, present her arguments rationally. Unfortunately, she didn't seem able to think in any sensible manner when she was around Alex.

That in itself was a good reason to run the other direction. *"You didn't come back, not for a long time."* Jason's plaintive voice echoed in her mind. No, she couldn't let him down. He needed someone, and she was the one he wanted right now.

Alex wasn't answering, and that fact jacked up

her tension level. He was probably trying to find a polite way to tell her he'd rather hire anyone else but her.

He walked to the other side of the long library table he used as a desk. It was littered with papers, and supported an elaborate computer system. Maybe he wanted to put some space between them, or maybe he was emphasizing the fact that this was his office, his house, his decision.

But there, beyond him, was the window seat where she'd curled up as a child. There, on the lowest shelf, were the storybooks she'd read. She had a place here, too.

He looked at her, a frown sending three vertical lines between his dark brows. "Are you sure this is something you want to do?"

She took a breath. At least he hadn't started with "no." Maybe he was willing to consider it. "Jason knows me, and Aunt Maida would feel better. I'm sure she'd call me five times a day from the hospital if the doctor would let her, just to be sure everything is all right."

"That's not what I asked." His gaze probed beneath the surface. "How do you feel about it, Paula?"

How did she feel about it? Mixed emotions—that was probably the best way to describe it. But Alex didn't need to know that. "I want the job. I think I can do it, although I don't have much experience." She remembered Aunt Maida's concerns, and plunged on. "I know you have some important entertaining coming up in the next month. If you're worried about that..."

What could she say? She couldn't claim expertise she didn't have. She'd never put on a fancy party in her life, and she didn't think her usual brand of entertaining was what Alex was used to. He'd probably never ordered in pizza for guests.

"I'm not." He glanced toward the portrait above the mantel, then away. "It's important, of course, but I'll hire a caterer for that, in any event. Maida's job would be to oversee the staff."

It sounded like a breeze compared to the elaborate cooking she'd been imagining. If someone else was doing the work, she ought to be able to manage a simple dinner party. "I think I could do that."

His gaze assessed her, and she stiffened. Maybe she hadn't lived all her life in a mansion, but she was smart enough to work her way through college. How hard could this be in comparison?

"Actually, that's not my concern at the moment." He looked impossibly remote, as if he viewed her through the wrong end of a telescope. "I want to know how you feel about working for me again, after what happened the last time you were here."

It was like a blow to the stomach, rocking her back on her heels. She hadn't dreamed he'd refer to it, had assumed he'd ignore what he probably saw as an unpleasant episode. Or that he'd forgotten it.

"That's all in the past," she said with as much firmness as she could manage. "You apologized. You said we'd pretend it never happened." He'd done a very good job of that, as she knew only too well. The humiliation she'd felt when he'd said those words brought a stinging wave of color to her cheeks. "Why are you bringing it up now?"

"Because I don't want it hanging between us," he said. "I don't want you to spend your time here worrying that I'll make the same mistake again."

A mistake, that's what it was to him. A moment of weakness when the moonlight had tricked him into a brief, romantic gesture he later regretted. Well, he was never going to know it meant any more than that to her.

"Please, forget about it." She forced herself to keep her voice steady and unconcerned. "I already have."

She had, of course. For nearly two years she'd forgotten it entirely. Maybe she'd have been better off if she'd never remembered. But just a week ago, the memory had popped out from behind the locked door in her mind. The doctors couldn't explain why. They'd said she could remember any time, or never.

She swallowed hard. What else might be hiding

there? She still didn't remember anything about those moments when the plane went down. Would she suddenly find herself reliving every painful second of the crash?

"Good." He was briskly businesslike. "In that case, we can start with a clean slate between us. If you're really willing to take on this position, it seems to be the best solution for everyone."

She tried to smile. *Position* was a fancy word for it. She was about to become an employee in his house. And she'd have to do it without ever letting him know how she felt about him.

"The best solution for everyone," she echoed. "We couldn't ask for better than that."

She had to find a way to keep her relationship with Alex businesslike—pleasant, but businesslike. She was just another employee to him, and as far as she was concerned, this was just another job. It was no different than if she'd been filing paperwork in someone's office.

Well, maybe a little different. If she were filing papers, she wouldn't be working for someone who tied her heart in knots.

Chapter Four

Paula put the carafe of coffee on a tray and glanced at the schedule Maida had taped to the kitchen cabinet, tension dancing along her nerves. Okay, so far she was on target, although it had probably taken her twice as long as it would have taken Maida. It was a good thing she'd decided to get up early this morning, Paula thought as she headed through the swinging door to the front of the house and up the stairs. Next on the agenda was to take the coffee to Alex's room.

The second-floor hallway was as big as the entire living room in the apartment she shared with another teacher back home. She pushed the thought away. If she let herself make comparisons like that, she'd be too intimidated to do her job.

She tapped first, then opened the heavy door—

more English oak. She remembered Maida showing her around the mansion on an earlier visit, explaining how one of Alex's ancestors had imported the paneling and brought artisans over from Germany to create the stained glass. Maida had been as proud as if it belonged to her.

"Paula, good." Alex strode into the bedroom from the bath, still buttoning his shirt. He stopped, looking at her. "Is something wrong?"

"No. Nothing." *Nothing except that I didn't anticipate how this much intimacy would affect me.* She forced down the flutter in her stomach and lifted the tray slightly. "Where would you like this?"

Instead of telling her, he took the tray, his hands brushing hers briefly. Her skin seemed sensitized to his touch, reacting with awareness in every cell. For an instant his gaze held hers. Was there more than business-as-usual in his eyes? Before she could be sure, he turned away and set the tray on the mahogany bureau. He busied himself pouring out a cup of coffee, his back to her.

She'd like to beat a retreat back to the kitchen, but Maida had said Alex would give his daily orders now. *Orders.* Paula swallowed a lump of resentment. She didn't take orders well; she never had. But she couldn't argue with Alex the way she would have with her father or brothers. In this situation, he was the boss, just as he had been when she was Jason's nanny. Their kiss hadn't changed that.

She pulled a pad and pencil from her jeans pocket. She'd taken the precaution of coming prepared, and the sooner this was done, the sooner she could escape. But Alex didn't seem to be in any hurry.

"Do you have some instructions for the day?" she prompted. Somehow "instructions" sounded fractionally better than "orders."

He glanced toward her, the lines around his dark eyes crinkling a little as he gestured with his coffee cup. "Let me get some of this down first. Then I'll be able to think."

She nodded, glad he couldn't know how dry her mouth felt at the moment. This was just too awkward—standing in Alex's private sanctum, watching him drink his morning coffee, noticing the way his dark hair tumbled over his forehead before he'd smoothed it back for the day. But she didn't have a choice.

She forced herself to stand still, glancing around the room to keep from staring at him. The heavy forest-green drapes and equally heavy mahogany furniture darkened the room, and the deep burgundy tones of the oriental carpet didn't help to brighten it. The room looked like a period set, in a museum. In fact, it probably was a period piece, but in a private home. She doubted that the furniture had been changed in several generations.

Had Alex had a colorful little boy's bedroom once, like Jason's? She smiled at the thought. She'd have to ask Maida. Somehow the idea of Alex with a cowboy or astronaut bedspread made him seem more like a regular person, instead of the blue blood who always stood slightly apart from the crowd.

Alex's cup clattered onto the tray, and he swung toward her. "Now, about the day's schedule—" His tone was businesslike, and her image of a little-boy Alex vanished.

"You'll need to see to Jason and the meals, of course. I won't be home for lunch, but I expect him to have a balanced meal. I'm sure Maida's talked to you about all that, hasn't she?"

"Yes." She tried to match his briskness. This was what she'd wanted, wasn't it? Brisk and businesslike, so she wouldn't imagine things she couldn't have. "And I have her schedule of the daily work, and when the cleaners and gardeners come." She poised the pencil over the pad. "I just need any special instructions."

"Hand me that tie, please."

For a split second she stared at the pad, confused, then realized what he meant. She took the striped tie from the dresser and handed it to him. He knotted it expertly, barely glancing in the mirror.

"Today I think it best if you concentrate on Jason. He's bound to feel a little apprehensive about Maida's absence. Try to keep him occupied.''

He held out his hand. This time she'd caught on, and she had the suit coat ready to put into it. Again their hands touched, and a faint tingle warmed her fingers. She snatched her hand away quickly.

''I may bring a business contact back to the house this afternoon,'' he went on, ''so please be sure there's coffee brewed and some sort of savories ready.''

Her mind went blank. ''Savories?''

''Cheese puffs, that sort of thing. Maida always serves something with coffee when people are here.'' He picked up his briefcase.

Pretzels or cookies probably weren't what he had in mind, she decided. ''I'll see what I can do.''

''I'll need you to pick up some dry-cleaning—'' He was already out the door, and she hurried to follow.

''You can do that when you go to visit Maida. And don't forget to check on shirts to go to the laundry.''

She scribbled on the pad, trailing him down the stairs. *Jason, dry-cleaning, laundry, coffee.* What else? Oh, yes, the savories, whatever they were going to be. Maybe she'd been just a bit optimistic in thinking this would be a breeze.

Alex stopped at the bottom of the steps, turning

suddenly. Their faces were on a level, only inches apart. Her breath caught.

"And tomorrow morning the coffee could be a little stronger."

"Stronger, right."

He turned away, heading for the dining room. She started to breathe again. So much for her idea that working for Alex could ever be cool and businesslike.

She'd really ended up with the worst of both worlds, she realized. As Alex's housekeeper, she would be in as close contact with him as a member of the family. But Alex would treat her like a servant, because in his eyes that was all she was.

Alex pulled into the driveway, sending a swift glance toward his passenger. He couldn't go so far as to say Conrad Klemmer's visit had gone well. The representative of the Swiss firm had been stiff, even seeming a little uncomfortable. Perhaps finishing their discussions in Alex's home would loosen him up a little.

It had better. Alex's stomach tightened. With any luck, a pleasant meeting in the library, sipping coffee and eating Maida's cheese straws—

But Maida wasn't here. Paula, quite aside from the totally inappropriate feelings she'd roused in him, was an unknown quantity when it came to running the house. This morning, in his bedroom, she'd seemed off balance. Or maybe he was projecting his own feelings onto her. It had certainly unsettled him to have Paula bringing him his coffee, handing him his tie. He hadn't anticipated the effect on him when she'd come in with his morning tray instead of Maida. He'd tried to act as if it were business as usual, but he probably hadn't succeeded.

Klemmer leaned forward, scanning the mansion from its pillared portico to the octagonal cupola on top.

"You have a lovely home," he commented in British-accented English. He glanced beyond the house, where the thickly wooded hillside swept sharply up to a saddleback ridge. "And a wonderful view."

"Thank you." Alex pulled to a stop and opened the door, surveying the landscape for any disorder and finding none. "We can finish our conversation in greater comfort here. My housekeeper should have some coffee ready for us."

He hoped. He led the way along the walk skirting the bank of rhododendrons, still heavily laden with flowers, that screened the front of the house from view. This meeting would be successful when he had a commitment from Klemmer to bring a full team in to negotiate the deal. Until then, the whole thing could fizzle away into nothing, and his last, best hope of saving the company would be gone.

"I'll get it!"

The shout from the front lawn startled him. They rounded the corner. Paula backpedaled toward them, a fielder's mitt extended. A baseball soared over her head.

He reached for the ball, seeing disaster in the making. He was a second too late. Klemmer caught it.

Paula, wearing her usual jeans and a T-shirt, skidded to a stop inches from them. Beyond her, Jason stood holding a bat, looking horrified.

They ought to be embarrassed. This was hardly the impression he'd expected to make on Klemmer. And it certainly wasn't the welcome he'd told Paula to prepare.

"I'm so sorry." She burst out, her cheeks scarlet. "I didn't mean... We were just practicing a little hitting."

"So I see." He bit off a retort. He couldn't say the words that crowded his tongue. Maybe that was just as well.

Klemmer was already reaching out to shake hands. "What a pleasure to meet your lovely family. This must be Mrs. Caine. I am Conrad Klemmer, your husband's business associate."

He wouldn't have thought it possible for Paula's flush to deepen, but it did.

"No, I—"

"Paula is my housekeeper." He kept his voice calm with an effort. "And this is my son, Jason."

Fortunately Jason remembered his manners. He dropped the bat, came quickly to them and extended his hand.

"How do you do, sir."

Klemmer darted a quick, speculative glance at Paula. Then he smiled. "It's a pleasure to meet both of you."

That speculative look only added more fuel to Alex's anger.

"Jason, will you show Mr. Klemmer to the library? I want to speak with Paula for a moment."

Jason nodded. "This way." He scampered up the steps and opened the door. "I'll show you."

The instant the door closed behind them, Alex turned to Paula, anger making his voice cold.

"Is this your idea of entertaining my business associate?"

"No, this is my idea of entertaining your son." Her green eyes sparked with answering anger. "That was my priority for today, remember?"

There might be some justice in her comment, but he was too annoyed to admit it at the moment. "I distinctly remember telling you I might be bringing an important business associate back with me this afternoon. I didn't expect you to greet him with a fly ball."

He saw her stubborn jaw tighten. "The coffee is

ready, and I found some of Maida's cheese straws in the freezer. Why shouldn't I play ball with Jason?''

''I don't care what you play with Jason,'' he ground out. ''But the back lawn is the appropriate place for baseball, not the front. Jason should know that, even if you don't.''

He knew how condescending it sounded the instant the words were out. But before he could say anything else, Paula had turned toward the door.

''I'll bring your coffee to the library.'' The words were coated with ice. ''It will just be a moment.''

The library. Klemmer. Alex followed her quickly. The Swiss businessman had to be his major concern right now. He had to salvage what was left of this meeting, if he could.

Then he'd worry about straightening things out with Paula. He wasn't sure which of those would be the more difficult.

Paula resisted the urge to clatter the baking sheet as she pulled cheese straws from the oven. That would be immature and childish. But it would feel so satisfying.

Using a spatula, she slid the straws onto a wire rack to cool for a moment before she took them in to the library. The cheese straws weren't the only things that needed to cool off. If she didn't get her temper under control, she wouldn't dare face Alex and Mr. Klemmer.

Well, she had every right to be angry. Alex had spoken to her as if she were beneath his consideration. As if only a barbarian would play catch with a child on the front lawn.

A reluctant smile tugged at her lips. Alex should see her neighborhood. Kids played ball anywhere and everywhere, including in the street.

The smile faded. Things were different here. She'd known that from the start. She'd known, too, that it was her responsibility to fit into Alex's world, and not the other way around.

Maybe, if she'd stopped to think about it, she'd have realized that the manicured front lawn wasn't intended for a game of catch. But it had been the first thing she'd suggested all day that brought a spark of enthusiasm to Jason's eyes, and she couldn't ignore that.

She wouldn't apologize for it, either. She arranged the coffee and cheese straws on a heavy silver tray, then picked the tray up, suppressing a nervous flutter in her stomach. She'd show Alex that she could be the perfect housekeeper, if that was what he wanted. But she wouldn't apologize for playing with his son. Jason could use a bit more play in his life.

The militant mood carried her down the hallway and right up to the library door. Then she paused, again needing to push down the apprehension that danced along her nerves. If Alex was still angry...well, he'd just have to get over it. She was doing her job. She tapped lightly, then opened the door.

The two men sat in the leather armchairs on either side of the fireplace. Was it just her imagination, or did Alex look worried?

She dismissed the thought. Alex, with his air of always being in perfect control, didn't worry about anything.

"Just put the tray here, please." Alex nodded to the inlaid coffee table between them.

She set the tray down, sensing Alex's quick assessment of it. Apparently satisfied, he nodded.

She poured the coffee into fragile china cups, careful not to let even a drop fall on the gleaming surface of the table. It wasn't until both men were served and she took a step back that she realized she'd been holding her breath.

Ridiculous, she scolded herself. She was being ridiculous to put so much pressure on herself to do this perfectly. And equally silly to imagine Alex would notice, or care.

"Will there be anything else?" she asked.

"That's fine, Paula." Alex's tone was cool and dismissive.

Well, all right. She could take a hint. Maybe he

expected her to bow her way out of his presence, like a servant of a medieval king.

She nodded briskly and spun away. The sooner she got out of here, the better. If they wanted more coffee, they could pour it themselves.

A couple of hours later, she hadn't exactly forgotten her irritation as she started supper, but it had been reduced to a slow simmer. Cooking, she'd discovered, was good for her disposition. Intent on Maida's chicken casserole recipe, she heard the kitchen door swing open. She turned, expecting Jason. But it was Alex, apparently back from delivering Klemmer to his hotel.

Her temper bubbled up again, as if their disagreement had been moments ago instead of an hour ago. "If you're here to deliver a lecture, don't bother." She dried her hands on a linen tea towel.

"Lecture?" His dark brows arched. "What lecture did you have in mind?"

"I got the message. No ball playing on the front lawn."

He held up his hands as if surrendering. "No lectures, I promise. I just came in to see if you had any more hot coffee."

The mild response took the wind out of her sails. It was tough to stay angry with someone who seemed to have forgotten the quarrel. She managed a smile. "This is a Norwegian kitchen, remember? There's always coffee."

Alex took a heavy white mug from the shelf and filled it. He took a long swallow, then stood staring down at the mug. "I owe you an apology."

That was the last thing she'd expected to hear him say, and it left her momentarily speechless.

He turned toward her, the faintest of smiles curving his firm lips. "I take it you agree."

"I..." She didn't seem to have anything to say. Her anger had slid away, and she didn't know what to replace it with. Maybe it was easier to hold on to the anger, because it provided a protection from feelings she didn't want to recognize. "You don't need to apologize to me. I work for you. If you have a problem with what I'm doing, you have to tell me."

He leaned back against the counter, and the lines of worry in his face were unmistakable. She'd told herself the richest man in town didn't have anything to worry about, but clearly she'd been wrong.

"The point is, I hadn't told you not to play ball on the front lawn. And I certainly shouldn't have spoken to you so sharply." He shook his head. "It wasn't your fault."

She wanted to tell him that it wasn't anybody's fault, that it was perfectly normal for a little boy to play ball on his own front lawn, but she couldn't. Obviously what was normal in her world wasn't in his.

"I hope your guest wasn't upset." She tried a smile. "At least I didn't give him a concussion."

Alex's face relaxed a fraction. "Thanks to his quick reflexes. I hadn't warned him he'd need a batting helmet when he came."

"Seriously, if you think I should apologize to him, I will." And what had happened to her fine conviction that she didn't owe anyone an apology?

"Not necessary. He has other things on his mind, anyway."

She wondered if expressing concern was beyond the limits of her job. "You look as if you do, too."

For a moment she thought he'd tell her it wasn't her business, but then he shrugged.

"Is it that obvious?"

"Pretty much." She could hardly say that she'd made a profession of studying him the last time she was here, or that she still remembered his every mood as if it had been yesterday.

"I suppose…" He frowned, then shook his head. "Maybe it's best if you know what's going on. What did Maida tell you?"

That Jason was lonely. That you were lonely. No, she couldn't say that, either. "About the business? She said you had some big deal going on, something that would happen this summer. She was worried about entertaining the visitors."

"I wish that were all I had to worry about." The

lines between his brows deepened, and again she had that ridiculous longing to smooth them away.

"What is it, then?" It had to be something serious, to make him look like that.

"If this deal doesn't go through—" He paused as if he didn't want to say anything else. "If it doesn't, I'm going to lose the company."

"But..." She grappled with the idea, trying to get her mind around it. It seemed impossible. "But you've always been the biggest employer in the county. How could this happen?"

"Changing markets, bad decisions." His face was grim. "It doesn't take much, not in today's economy. If this deal with Dieter Industries goes through, it will open up a whole new marketing opportunity for us. If not, the company will go under."

"But so many people count on Caine Industries." That probably wasn't the most comforting thing she could have said.

"Half the town." His hand tightened on the coffee mug until the knuckles turned white. "Half the town directly, and more than that indirectly. If I can't pull off this deal, I'll let all of them down."

The pain he was trying to hide caught at her heart. "It's not just your responsibility. There are other people involved. No one will blame you."

He shot her a skeptical glance. "You can't believe that, Paula. If Caine Industries goes under,

everyone will blame me—most of all I will blame
me. And there won't be a company to leave to my
son.''

She didn't have any words to deal with something like this. Apparently the prince in his castle
wasn't safe from the world's problems, after all.

"I'm sorry," she said at last.

He shrugged, pushing away from the counter. "I
thought you should know what's at stake, because
you're a part of it. These people from Dieter have
to be entertained, and they expect it to be in my
home. That means you have to keep things running
properly.''

No more ball games on the front lawn, in other
words. Why hadn't Maida explained all this to her?
Because she'd been afraid Paula would run at the
thought of it?

Or because she knew one little boy was in danger
of getting lost in the midst of all this high-powered
business.

Paula realized Alex was waiting for some response from her. She looked up, meeting his gaze.
"I'll do my best," she said. *My best for Jason, and
for you.*

Chapter Five

⟋

The prince in the castle, the man who had everything, stood on the verge of losing it all. *No, not all,* Paula corrected herself, drying the silverware from breakfast the next morning. The Caine family fortune would probably survive the loss of the company that bore its name. But for a proud, private man like Alex, the blow would still be severe. When he'd said there might be no company to leave to his son, she'd glimpsed a secret agony in his eyes that he probably didn't guess he'd revealed.

He wouldn't like it that he'd exposed so much of his inner life to her. She knew that instinctively. He wasn't a man who confided his troubles willingly or easily. Probably no one in Bedford Creek understood just how important this business deal of Alex's was to all of them.

Paula stared absently out at the June sunlight slanting over the mountain, gilding the pool. Aunt Maida didn't know how crucial it was. She'd never have kept that from Paula. *"Take care of Jason."* Maida's voice rang in Paula's mind. *"Find out what's bothering that child."*

Paula found herself counting the number of times Jason had smiled. Twice the day before, when they'd been playing ball. Once today, when she'd made a happy face with syrup on his pancake.

She clasped wet hands on the edge of the sink. *Dear Father, if Maida's right, if you do have something for me to do here, please show me my task.*

"Washing-up prayers," Maida called them. She always said she could feel as close to God standing at the sink as she could in church.

Movement on the patio caught Paula's eye. Alex skirted the pool, then headed for the empty cottage the gardener had occupied, back in the days when estates like this one had live-in gardeners. As she watched from the window, he opened the door and went inside.

She'd probably never have a better chance to catch him where Jason couldn't overhear. Maybe God was answering her prayer already, giving her an opportunity to talk to Alex about Jason's needs. She dried her hands and hurried out the back.

Curiosity overtook her as she approached the cottage. What had brought Alex here? She knocked.

The door swung open promptly, but before she could see inside, Alex's tall frame blocked the space.

"Paula." He didn't sound particularly welcoming. "I'm rather busy. Can this wait?"

"I'd like to talk with you before you leave for the plant. May I come in?"

She took a step toward the door. Alex didn't back away. Instead, he stood like a solid barrier, his frown a warning signal.

"We can discuss whatever it is this evening. I really don't have time now." His tone suggested that anything she might wish to discuss was far less important than his agenda.

She fought to control her temper. She wanted to involve him in making plans for Jason, not alienate him. "I want to talk with you about Jason, and I'd like to do it where there's no chance he'll overhear." Again she made a slight movement toward the door, and again his immobility stopped her. For a moment he just looked at her, frowning.

Then he stepped out of the cottage and pulled the door closed behind him. She heard a lock snap.

She lifted her eyebrows. "I wasn't planning to break in. You didn't need to lock it."

His frown deepened. "I keep some plans I'm working on in there," he said. "The office stays locked so they won't be disturbed."

In other words, he didn't get away from work

even when he was at home. She wondered if he had any idea just how compulsive that sounded.

He took her arm, leading her a few steps away from the cottage, and her skin warmed as if she'd walked into the sunlight.

"All right, what's so important?" He shot back his shirtsleeve to consult his watch. "I have to be down at the plant in less than half an hour."

"I want to talk with you about Jason."

"You already said that. What about Jason?" That faintly defensive tone she'd noticed before threaded his voice.

Carefully, she thought. Say this carefully. "I'm a little concerned about him. I know this is a difficult time for him with Maida in the hospital, but he seems so withdrawn."

"Withdrawn?" She had the sense that his muscles tightened. Hers seemed to clench, too, as if preparing to fight or run. "My son is not withdrawn."

She tried to force herself to relax, tried to smile. "You make it sound like a communicable disease."

He didn't smile back.

"Alex, I'm just afraid he's worrying too much about things, instead of talking them over with people he trusts."

"You can't expect him to trust you immediately. He probably barely remembers you from the last time you were here."

"I realize that." *Even though I remember him, and you, as if it were yesterday.* "I didn't necessarily mean me. Is he talking to you about Maida, or about anything else that worries him?"

His face hardened. "I've already told you, I don't think it's wise to discuss illness with him. I don't want him to worry—that's why I protect him from such things."

"But—"

"He is my son, Paula. These decisions are mine to make, and I'm raising Jason the best way I know. Now if that's all, I really have to get to the plant."

She was losing him, losing the chance to make him see that Jason needed something he wasn't getting from the people in his life. There had to be something, some positive step she could take right now for that child. Maybe it was time, as her brother Keith, the football player, would say, to drop back and punt.

"What about his friends?" She blurted the words out before Alex could walk away. "I haven't seen any of Jason's friends since I've been here."

"You've only been here a couple of days." He looked harassed, as if she were a small dog nipping at his heels. "Jason has friends."

"Where are they? Wouldn't it be good for him to be playing with them every day to distract him from Maida's absence?" She had to press whatever advantage she had.

"He has friends at school."

"It's summer vacation. What does he do for friends during the summer?"

Alex gave an exasperated sigh. "We don't exactly have neighbors to run in and out, Paula."

True enough. The Caine mansion, sitting on land that seemed carved out of the hillside above the town, was alone and isolated. A steep, winding lane led from the mansion to the nearest street, far below.

"Then we ought to be making an effort to get him together with his friends, even if I have to drive him. Don't you agree?" A plan, somewhat hazy and amorphous, began to take shape in her mind.

"Yes, I suppose so." He took a step away. "Look, I have to go. You're right, Jason needs to see his friends. I'll trust you to arrange it. Do whatever you think is best."

She nodded, the plan becoming clearer by the moment. "You can count on it," she said, watching as he strode away, obviously eager to get to work. Well, she was just as eager to get to her work, now that he'd given her a green light.

Alex might be a little surprised when he found out what she thought was best for his son—and maybe for him, too.

He had just enough time to swim his laps before dinner, Alex decided as he arrived home that afternoon. He tried to ignore the pain that radiated down his leg, but it demanded attention. He might succeed in denying weakness to everyone else, but he couldn't deny it to himself.

Too much stress, too little exercise. He knew exactly what Brett would say, whether he spoke as a doctor or a friend. And Brett would be right. Alex had too many people depending on him to let physical weakness get in the way of doing what he had to do.

"Jason?" He called as he entered the center hallway, but no one answered. Perhaps Jason and Paula had gone somewhere.

He started upstairs to change, trying to push away memories of that conversation with her that morning. She'd been persistent, he'd give her that. Her face, intent and serious, formed in his mind before he could block it out. In fact, her presence seemed to linger in the house even when she wasn't here, refusing to leave him alone.

All right, he was too aware of Paula Hansen. He accepted that, he admitted it. But that didn't mean he was going to act on it. There wasn't room in his life right now for anything other than his son and the business deal that might save them. His relationship with Paula would stay strictly business. That was what he'd promised her, and that was the way it would be.

Ten minutes later, towel over his arm, he walked

out to the pool area. Paula and Jason hadn't gone anywhere; they were in the pool.

Paula glanced up, saw him and waved. Sunlight glinted on her blond hair and turned her warm skin golden. She wore a green swimsuit that matched her eyes. He swallowed with difficulty.

Hiding any suggestion of a limp, he crossed to the pool.

"This is a surprise. Jason doesn't usually like the water."

"Sure I do, Dad," Jason said quickly. But the tight grip he had on Paula's hand gave him away.

"If you want us to get out..." Paula began.

"No, of course not." He dropped the towel and stepped into the water. "There's plenty of room for all of us. I'd better get my laps in before Brett Elliot sends the exercise police after me."

Her face relaxed in a smile. "He is a good doctor, isn't he. He's been in to see Maida so much, and every time it perks her up."

"He cares." He could say more, could tell her how only Brett's determined intervention had brought him as far as he'd come in recovering from the effects of the crash.

He could, but why would he? Where had it come from, this longing to confide in Paula? She was his housekeeper. Listening to his personal troubles wasn't part of her job description.

"Well, I'd better get at it." He turned away

quickly, before he could give in to the impulse to share anything else with Paula. Before he could let his gaze linger on her smooth, honey-colored skin or the freckles that splashed across her cheeks.

Stroke, kick, stroke, kick. The familiar pattern soothed him, and he felt tight muscles gradually relax, responding to the repetitive motion and the massage of the water. When he swam, he could block out everything but the movement and the water.

At least, usually he could. Somewhere about the fifteenth lap, he realized that he wasn't letting his mind float clear. He was listening to Paula and his son.

She seemed to be coaxing Jason to trust the water to hold him up. If she succeeded, she'd be doing a better job than Alex ever had. He'd tried to get his son interested in swim lessons, but Jason had always held back. He'd finally realized the boy was afraid, and he hadn't known quite what to do about it. His own father would have bullied him into conquering the fear, but that wasn't the way he wanted to raise Jason.

"There, see?" Paula had kicked off and pushed herself through the water to Jason, then grabbed his hands. "I trust you to catch me. You want to try it?"

Alex stood at the shallow end of the pool, half

turned away from them, not wanting Jason to think he had an audience, and listened.

"I guess so."

Jason sounded reluctant. Alex wanted to intervene, wanted to tell Paula not to push the boy. But just this morning he'd told her to do what she thought was best for Jason. He shouldn't second-guess her already.

He glanced toward them. Paula didn't even seem to notice that he was there. All her attention was focused on his son. Her smile encouraged Jason, and she held out her hands to him.

"I won't let you sink, honest. I promise."

Jason nodded, shivering a little as a breeze swept across the pool. Alex saw his skinny chest rise as he took a breath. Then, his gaze fixed on Paula's face as if it were a lifeline, Jason launched himself through the water.

"All right!" Paula grabbed his hands and helped him upright. "You did it, Jason. And you didn't sink one little bit."

"I did it, didn't I." Jason grinned. "I really did it."

"Good job, Jason." There was, unaccountably, a lump in Alex's throat, along with maybe the smallest bit of jealousy that Jason had tried for Paula something he'd never tried for his father.

Jason glanced at him, startled, as if he'd forgotten

his father was in the pool. Paula held out her hand, inviting Alex to join them.

"Maybe Jason will float to you, if you promise not to let him sink." The faintest stress suggested that *promise* was the operative word.

Alex didn't need Paula to tell him how to react to his own son. He hoped his look made that clear. "Jason knows he can trust me." He held out his hands. "Come on, Jason."

His son seemed to mentally figure the distance between them. "Come a little bit closer, Dad."

He almost coaxed Jason to try it, but Paula's eyes held a warning that might as well have been shouted. He swallowed his resentment and took a giant step forward. "How's that?"

"Okay." Jason bounced a little, as if working up his nerve. Then he pushed off, face screwed up, hands reaching toward Alex.

Alex grabbed him. "Way to go, son." He grasped a small, wet shoulder. "Good job."

Jason looked up at him, all the reserve gone from his dark eyes, at least for the moment. "I did it!" He turned, reaching out for Paula, and she swam a stroke or two closer to take his hand.

"You sure did." She stood, water streaming from sun-warmed skin, and smiled at them.

The smile went straight to Alex's heart and lodged there, making one thing abundantly clear. Ignoring Paula would not be an easy thing to do.

* * *

Paula's breath caught in her throat. Did Alex have any idea how devastatingly attractive he looked at that moment? He and Jason wore identical, laughing expressions and the tenderness in his gaze when he looked at his son made her want to cry. As for the expression in his eyes when he looked at her—no, she must be imagining that.

She had to keep her mind on her job. Right now, that meant unlocking the puzzle that was Jason, and part of the answer had just played itself out right in front of her. One of the things Jason needed, maybe the most important thing, was a closer relationship with his father.

She didn't doubt that Alex loved his son—loved him more than life itself, probably. He just didn't seem to know how important it was for a seven-year-old to feel love, not just hear the word. If only Alex were willing to listen to her, she could help him understand.

"Alex, I—"

The telephone rang, so close it startled her. Then, as Alex turned and swung out of the pool, she realized he'd brought his cellular phone out with him.

"Just one minute," he said, drying his hand and then picking up the phone.

In an instant she knew that playtime in the pool was over as far as Alex was concerned. His gaze turned inward as he concentrated on the call, and she could almost see him donning his corporate armor. Without looking back at them, still talking, he went into the house.

She tried to swallow her disappointment. Alex had business to take care of; she could understand that. It didn't have to spoil Jason's afternoon. She held out her hand to the boy.

"How about another try, Jason?"

But all the interest and happiness had gone out of Jason's small face. Shivering, he climbed out of the pool. "Don't want to."

"We don't have to go in yet," she said. "We could play a game of water polo."

"I don't like water polo." He grabbed a towel and started for the house. "I don't like swimming at all." He ran inside, slamming the door behind him.

Paula climbed slowly out of the pool. Jason might say he didn't like swimming, but she had a pretty clear idea what was bothering him. And it had much more to do with his father than with the pool.

She toweled her hair, feeling it curl over her fingers as it began to dry. She'd look like a poodle if she didn't blow-dry it, but she probably should have started dinner already. She pulled on her terry robe and headed for the kitchen.

Paula had no sooner gotten in the back door than Alex came hurrying toward her. Somehow he'd found time to pull on jeans and a knit shirt, and his dark hair was slicked back, still damp from the shower.

"Paula, thank you. That's the most interest Jason has ever shown in swimming. I'd about given up."

She clutched the robe around her, embarrassingly aware of how disheveled she must look. "I'm glad." She edged past him. "I really have to get changed and start dinner."

He shook his head, smiling. "Why are you embarrassed? I saw you in your swimsuit in the pool."

She didn't know why there was a difference between playing in the swimming pool with Jason and standing so close to Alex in the narrow hallway, but there was. And she didn't intend to say that to him.

"It's not that," she said. "I just don't want dinner to be late." She managed a smile. "My boss might not like that."

He touched a wet curl, turning it around his finger. His hand came within a millimeter of her cheek, and her skin tingled as if he'd caressed it. "Right now, your boss is very happy with you." His tone teased her. "You could probably burn the biscuits, and he wouldn't say a thing."

She wanted so badly to lean toward him. Just the slightest movement would bring them together. Her treacherous memory told her exactly how his hand would feel against her face.

She stepped back, instead. "I'll remind you of

that when I put dinner in front of you. Now, I really need to get started.''

His hand closed around her wrist. "Just one second. I wanted to tell you that your success in the pool with Jason gave me an idea for something that might make this time a bit better for him.''

"That's great.'' Was she really going to get her wish so easily? Had Alex seen how much it meant to Jason when the boy felt his father's encouragement?

"One of the high school coaches gives swimming lessons to kids in the summer. I hadn't even considered hiring him, since Jason wasn't interested, but now I think that's just the thing.''

"Swimming lessons?'' Her heart fell. Jason didn't need lessons from a stranger. He needed his father.

"It's perfect. Lessons will give him something to think about and keep his mind off Maida.''

"Alex, I'm not sure that's what Jason needs right now. Maybe it would be better if you taught him.''

"Me?'' He looked at her as if she were crazy. "I don't have time to do that now. Besides, kids usually learn better from someone other than a parent.''

"Jason was excited because you were there. I'm not sure he'd be equally happy about swimming with someone else.'' In fact, given the way the child had left the pool, she was sure he wouldn't.

But Alex wasn't listening. He turned, headed toward the front of the house. "I'll try and reach him now. Thanks, Paula."

"Alex, I don't think…"

It was too late. He'd already charged through the swinging door.

Typical, so very typical. If Alex approached his business with that energy and directness, he'd undoubtedly saved the company several times over. He hadn't even heard anything she'd said.

She ran her hand through wet curls, seeming to feel again Alex's gentle touch. She forced her mind away from that moment in which they'd stood so close. She couldn't afford to let herself think about that.

She'd asked God to show her what she was supposed to be doing. And now God had given her the answer, in language so clear she couldn't possibly ignore it.

God had given her a chance to make up for the mistakes she'd made the last time she was here. Maybe that was why her memories had come back when they had. God had known she'd need them to accomplish her task.

No matter how difficult it was, she'd have to put her own needs and feelings aside for the time being. She had to help bring the prickly, private father and son closer together. And she suspected she really had her work cut out for her.

Chapter Six

"Are you sure this is going to be all right with my dad?" Jason's dark eyes filled with concern the next afternoon.

Paula tried to push down her matching concern and speak with a confidence she didn't feel. "Your dad won't care one way or the other if I have a pet in the cottage. And I need something to keep me company while Aunt Maida is in the hospital." She opened the door to the animal shelter. "Come on. You've got to help me pick out just the right puppy."

The long room was filled with kennels on either side, and their entry signaled a chorus of yips and howls. Every dog there seemed to be proclaiming, *Pick me, pick me!*

"So many dogs." Jason's tone was awed. "How can you decide?"

She ruffled his hair. "That's why you're along. When we find the right one, we'll know."

And when Alex found out about this, what would he think? She tried to assure herself that what she'd said to Jason was true. Technically, this puppy was going to be hers, at least until Alex saw that it made a difference in his son's life.

Besides, he'd said she should use her own judgment about getting Jason together with friends. Somehow she felt a puppy might be just the right friend for Jason now—a creature that would depend on him and love him unconditionally.

And if she ended up having to take the dog back to Baltimore, she'd deal with that when the time came. But with that in mind, maybe a small breed would be best. She could just imagine what her roommate would say if she came home with a huge dog.

"Oh, Paula, look." Jason leaned against a large pen filled with puppies of every description, all barking and tumbling over each other.

The attendant smiled. "Shall I let the two of you into the puppy pen to make your choice?"

Paula tried to dismiss the image of Alex's frowning face. "Let's do it."

They were engulfed in a melee of puppies the instant they entered the pen. Laughing, Paula removed a beagle from her shoe. The little cocker spaniel might work. It shouldn't get too big. She looked at Jason. "What do you think?"

Jason was on his knees. A fluffy yellow pup had planted suspiciously large paws on his shoulder and was licking his face. The boy looked up, his eyes filled with longing that clutched her heart and wouldn't let go. "This one, Paula. Please, this has to be the one."

"What is it?" she asked the attendant, a sense of foreboding filling her.

The girl grinned. "A yellow Labrador. Great dogs."

"Large dogs." She banished Alex's face firmly from her mind. "Okay. He's the one." Jason's joy was worth any number of confrontations with his father.

A few hours later, she wasn't so sure. She hurried to finish dinner preparations, her stomach tied in knots over Alex's impending return. Jason and the puppy, playing on the kitchen floor, slowed her down, but she didn't feel comfortable letting them out of her sight yet.

She scooped the puppy out of her way as she bent to open the oven door. "Here, Jason. Keep him away from the hot stove. We don't want him to get hurt." She lifted out the casserole dish. "Have you thought of a good name yet?"

Jason frowned, forehead wrinkling in an imitation of his father. "Goldy would be nice, 'cause of his color. But that sounds like a girl's name, and he might not like that."

She suppressed a smile. "What about Nugget? You know, like a gold nugget."

"Nugget." He tried the name, then tickled the puppy. "You like that, boy? You want to be Nugget?"

The puppy wiggled, licking his face.

"He likes it!" Jason declared. "His name is Nugget."

Paula's heart turned over at the sheer happiness in his face. She hadn't seen Jason look like that since she'd come here. His closed-off, somber expression had vanished. Now he looked like any normal seven-year-old should. Surely Alex would see that and would understand what she was trying to do.

"I'm going to carry this into the dining room." She picked up the casserole dish. "You hold Nugget so he doesn't get out."

Two things happened at once. Paula pushed through the door between the kitchen and the dining room, and Jason lost his hold on the puppy's collar. Paula felt a brush of fur against her legs, then lifted the casserole out of the way as Jason charged after the puppy.

"Grab him, Jason!" She deposited the casserole

dish on the waiting trivet and dived after the golden blur. "Don't let him get out."

She skidded across the marble floor of the hallway in Jason's wake. Her feet tangled with the throw rug; she lost her balance and sat down heavily. Nugget danced just out of her reach—his paws scratching a pair of highly polished brown wingtips.

Alex, who'd just come in the front door, bent over and picked up the wriggling puppy. He held it at arm's length, and his expression looked just as ominous as she'd imagined it might.

"What, exactly, is this?"

The glib explanation she'd prepared died in her throat. "A puppy."

His frown deepened. "I can see that it's a puppy. Whose puppy is it, and what is it doing in my front hall?"

She scrambled to her feet, trying to find some reasonable words.

"He's Paula's, Dad." Jason gathered the fur ball carefully into his arms. "I helped her pick him out. His name is Nugget."

"Nugget." Alex's expression didn't lighten, but she thought she saw him ruffle the puppy's ears before he pinned her with that frowning gaze. "Tell me exactly why you need a dog *now*, of all times."

"Well, I..." All her assurance shriveled at that frown.

"Paula gets lonesome in the cottage by herself at night," Jason piped up. "She needs Nugget to keep her company."

"She does, does she?" Alex's gaze softened slightly as he looked at his son. "Well, why don't you take Nugget out on the lawn for a while. Paula and I have to talk."

"Okay." Laden down with puppy, Jason trudged to the swinging door. "I'll get his leash, Paula. And I'll be really careful."

"I know you will." Suppressing the urge to run out the door after them, she turned to Alex. "If there's a problem with my having a pet in the cottage…"

His dark brows lifted. "But he's not in the cottage, is he?"

She couldn't deny that. "He's so little, I didn't want to leave him alone. He and Jason were playing in the kitchen while I cooked supper. I never intended for him to get into this part of the house."

Alex leaned a little closer, and she had the sudden feeling that he was using up all the air in the hallway. How else could she explain her sudden breathlessness?

"You're lonely in the cottage at night?" His tone made it a question. "Ms. Independence, the woman who's not afraid of anything?"

She shrugged. "Everyone's afraid of something." *What are you afraid of, Alex, besides losing the company? What keeps those barriers between you and the rest of the world?*

He studied her, his gaze so probing that it was as if he could see right through her. "Who picked out the puppy?" he asked abruptly.

"Jason did."

He lifted an eyebrow. "I see. And who named the puppy?"

She had to stiffen her muscles to keep from fidgeting. "Jason and I both did."

"I see," he said again. His expression didn't change, but she realized that was amusement lurking in his dark eyes. She was right—he did look straight through her. At least he wasn't demanding she take the dog back.

"Really, Alex, he won't be any trouble at all," she said quickly. "I'll keep him out of your way. I promise." She held her breath.

"I did tell you to do whatever you thought best for my son, didn't I? But this wasn't quite what I had in mind."

She chose her words carefully, not wanting to imply that she knew better than he what Jason needed. "I just thought it might help to take his mind off things right now. There's nothing like a puppy for occupying a small boy."

A smile tugged the corners of his lips. "And then there's the little matter of keeping you company at night." His voice dropped. "We don't want you to get lonely."

"N-no I won't," she stammered. He was too close, way too close. With the spicy scent of his aftershave teasing her senses, she could hardly think coherently. She took a step back, putting some space between them. "And I will keep him out of your hair."

Alex gave a quick nod. "I don't like disorder in my life, Paula. See that the puppy doesn't bring any, and we'll both be happy."

She wanted to point out that disorder was a chronic and even desirable state when it came to puppies and small boys, but she was afraid to press her luck. At least Nugget could stay. "I'll see to it."

Alex stopped her as she started toward the kitchen. "One other thing, Paula. I have a church committee meeting here tonight at eight. I'd like you to serve coffee and dessert." He raised his eyebrows. "Unless you'll be busy puppy-sitting then."

"Coffee and dessert, right." Her mind scrambled among the possibilities, coming up empty. "I'll take care of it. And dinner will be ready in five minutes."

When Jason and the puppy came into the kitchen in answer to her call, she was frantically leafing through Maida's wooden recipe box. How could

Alex calmly expect dessert to be served to guests, just like that? What would her aunt have done?

"I'm ready for supper," Jason announced. "What are you doing?"

"Looking for a dessert I can fix in no time flat. Your dad wants me to serve something to a committee he has coming here tonight." She hoped she didn't sound as panicky as she felt. If she'd known ahead of time, if she hadn't spent the afternoon at the animal shelter...

Jason rinsed his hands at the sink. He grabbed for the tea towel and knocked the recipe box over.

Paula caught it. "Careful. I don't want that to get broken."

"It's just an old box. We could get Maida a new one."

"I couldn't do that." She ran her hand along the box's polished surface. "I gave this to Maida when I was about your age. I did chores for a month to earn enough money to buy it."

"Really?" The concept was obviously out of his experience.

"Really. And I hoped just now I'd find a fast, easy dessert recipe in it, but I didn't."

"Why don't you call Ingrid's?"

She looked at him blankly. "Who's Ingrid and how can she help?"

Jason giggled. "Ingrid's a bakery. It's the one Maida uses for stuff like that. You just call and tell them what you want, and they bring it to the house. Then you put it on a nice plate and serve it.''

You put it on a nice plate and serve it. ''That sounds like a terrific plan.'' Always assuming the bakery would still be open, of course. But during tourist season, every shop stayed open late. She wasn't sure whether she was happier over the answer to her problem or the fact that it had come from Jason. ''Thanks, Jason. You've really helped me.''

''It's okay.'' A faint flush colored his cheeks. He bent to say something to Nugget, then scurried into the dining room.

The puppy sat back on his haunches and stared at her, his tongue lolling in a silly doggy grin.

''I think we're making progress, Nugget,'' she told him.

With Jason, anyway. As for Alex... well, that was another story. The memory of those moments in the hallway flooded over her. If she could keep her feelings under control, she'd be better off. But that seemed impossible where Alex was concerned.

Alex pushed chairs into a semicircle in the library for the church fund-raising committee. He ought to be concentrating on the agenda for the meeting or on the appropriate amount for the donation he'd undoubtedly be expected to make. Instead, he was thinking about Paula.

Those moments in the hallway had gotten totally out of control. He seemed to stand back and look at himself in surprise. He'd been *flirting* with her—there was no other word that fit. It was the last thing in the world he should have been doing.

He saw again the wave of warm, peachy color filling her cheeks, saw the way her eyes sparked with indignation or clouded when she tried to think up a reasonable explanation for an unreasonable action.

He was spending entirely too much time thinking about Paula Hansen, he decided. All right, granted she had an appeal for him that he couldn't begin to explain. He still couldn't risk giving in to that attraction.

His mouth tightened. When his wife had walked away from their marriage and from their son, she'd made it clear that his small-town life wasn't what she'd expected from a rich man. He hadn't measured up for her, just as he'd never measured up for his father. He could accept that, and he could build a life without a romantic relationship.

And even if he wanted to expose himself to that kind of hurt again, he wouldn't risk Jason's happiness. His son had had too many people disappear from his young life. Jason wasn't going to be put in a position of learning to love someone and then having that someone leave.

Maybe Paula wouldn't leave, a treacherous voice whispered in his mind.

She did before, he reminded himself.

His rational side assured him this was the right decision. Anything between Paula and him had to be strictly business, for all their sakes. He'd put a guard on his emotions, and that little incident in the hallway wouldn't happen again.

The doorbell rang, and he went to let his guests in.

An hour later, the fund-raising committee had made progress on plans for the new campaign, and he had begun to wonder what had happened to Paula and the coffee. Almost as soon as the thought formed in his mind, the door opened. Paula, burdened with a large tray, entered.

"Why don't we take a break," he suggested. "I see Paula has brought some refreshments."

He had to smile. Paula, apparently determined to be the perfect hostess, had changed from her usual jeans to a skirt and blouse. He couldn't help noticing that the sunny yellow of the blouse brought out the gold flecks in her eyes.

You weren't going to notice things like that, he lectured himself. Before he could move, Mitch Donovan had leaped to his feet to take the tray from Paula.

"Let me give you a hand with that." Mitch balanced the tray while she cleared a spot for it on the cherry table against the wall. "It's good to see you again, Paula."

Paula looked a little startled at suddenly being the center of attention. Maybe it didn't fit in with her idea of a housekeeper's role. If so, she'd forgotten something about Bedford Creek, Alex thought.

"I think you know most of these people," Alex said. "You remember Gwen Forrester."

The older woman smiled. "How is Maida doing?" Her voice was warm with sympathy. "I just heard about her surgery. It's just like her to keep it a secret. She never wants to accept help. I plan to go and see her tomorrow, if you think she's ready for company."

Paula barely had time to nod before Pastor Richie interrupted. "I'm sure she'd love it, Gwen. I went in today but she'd like to see someone besides me. And Paula, of course."

"You know Pastor Simon Richie," Alex went on. He'd gotten used to interruptions with this group. "And you remember Mitch Donovan, our police chief."

Mitch smiled as he helped himself to a cup of coffee. "I remember Paula from when she was Jason's nanny."

"And this is Ellie Wayne, our church organist." As people got up and moved toward the coffee service, Alex introduced the last member of the committee. Ellie nodded, her wary manner with strangers disguising her generous heart.

"You'll be coming to worship with us on Sunday, I hope." Simon Richie sugared his coffee generously. "Maida never misses, and she'll want to know everything that happens."

Before Paula could respond, Gwen Forrester began giving her suggestions for Maida's therapy. Alex exchanged a smiling look with Mitch. Since Gwen's daughter had married Bedford Creek's only doctor, she had begun to consider herself an authority on all things medical.

Mitch crossed the room to join him. "Nice to have Paula back again, isn't it?" he said softly.

Alex tried for a neutral tone. "I'm sure it's eased Maida's mind, having her here."

"Maida's, huh." Mitch lifted a quizzical brow. "Actually, it wasn't Maida I had in mind."

Most people in Bedford Creek wouldn't probe into a Caine's personal affairs, but Mitch wasn't most people. He'd saved Alex's life, once upon a time. Maybe he felt that gave him the right to ask what others wouldn't.

"She's good with Jason," Alex said, gaze fixed on Paula. She was laughing at some comment of Simon's, and he felt a stab of what seemed like jealousy. "Irrational." He stiffened with annoyance when he realized he'd said it aloud.

Mitch eyed him with some amusement. "What's

irrational? The fact that she's good with Jason? Or are you talking about her effect on you?''

"Neither." He turned his back on the small group by the fireplace. "Paula's an employee, nothing more."

"Try that on someone who doesn't know you as well as I do," Mitch said. "You're attracted to her."

He knew Mitch would see through anything less than the truth. "I shouldn't be," he said.

"Why? She's free, you're free. There's no reason—"

"Alex!" Gwen's call was peremptory, and he swung toward her. "You have to convince Paula to come to the church picnic Saturday. After all, you and Jason are coming. She can come with you."

Paula's cheeks were flushed. "I'm not sure that's a good idea."

"Nonsense," Gwen said briskly, her gray curls bouncing with emphasis. "You'll have to fix something, anyway, so you might as well come and enjoy it."

Paula glanced at Alex, and he wasn't sure what was in her eyes. Embarrassment at being singled out? He spoke before the silence could become awkward. "We'd like to have you join us, if you want."

"There, that's settled." Gwen beamed. "I'm going to make my apple-crumb pies. Ellie, what are you bringing?''

Alex glanced toward Mitch, to find his old friend regarding him with amusement.

"Is that a date?" Mitch asked softly.

"Certainly not," he said. He saw Paula slipping out of the library and knew he had to speak with her before the situation became awkward. "Excuse me."

He caught up with Paula at the kitchen door. She looked at him somewhat distantly.

"Is there something else I can bring you?" she asked.

"What? No, that's fine." He frowned, not sure how to say what he felt he must. "Look, I know Gwen's friendliness can be a little overpowering at times. If you don't want to go to that picnic, you certainly don't have to. I can make some excuse."

She looked at him steadily for several moments, and for once her usually readable face didn't give anything away. "Does that mean you don't want me to go?"

"Of course not!" He always seemed to say the wrong thing to her. Or maybe she always took what he said the wrong way. He grasped her arm, and immediately knew he shouldn't have. He could feel her smooth skin warm at his touch. "Look, I didn't mean it that way at all. I just meant that you shouldn't feel obligated. It's not part of your job.

But Jason and I would enjoy having you come with us. Please.''

A dimple appeared at the corner of her mouth. ''I guess we should leave Nugget at home.''

''Definitely.'' He smiled. ''We'll give him a dog biscuit to make up for it.''

''It's a deal.'' Still smiling, she turned and disappeared through the swinging door.

He stood for a moment, not yet ready to go back in the library and face Mitch's inquisitive gaze. What exactly had just happened here? He'd intended to keep his distance from Paula. He'd assured himself that what happened before wouldn't happen again. And instead, he'd committed himself to a social event with her.

It's not a date, he repeated to himself. He was just being hospitable to someone who was, after all, a stranger here.

He had to believe that was all there was to it.

Chapter Seven

By the next afternoon, Paula had been over the events of the previous day a hundred times in her mind, and she was no closer to deciding what they meant. One moment Alex had barked orders at her, the next he'd seemed to want...what? Friendship? Something more? She just didn't know.

"Come on, kids." She waved to Jason and Kristie, Gwen Forrester's granddaughter; they were playing with Nugget on the lawn near the pool. "You can go back in the water now. Jason, better put Nugget in his pen."

Having Kristie join Jason's swim lessons had been a stroke of genius, if Paula did think so herself. If Alex wouldn't teach his son, at least Jason would have the company of a playmate. Kristie, a year younger than Jason, was quick and adventurous. She'd stayed after the lesson to play, with the promise that they'd go back in the pool again later in the afternoon.

Paula sat on the pool edge, dangling her feet in the water, and watched the children play with a float in the shallow end. Timing was everything, she decided. Alex had arrived home moments before, and, true to his routine, he was changing to swim his laps. When he got to the pool, he'd discover he had company.

She stretched, enjoying the sun's heat on her back. Maybe she couldn't, and probably shouldn't, do anything about Alex's attitude toward her. But she ought to be able to influence how he behaved with his son.

This will work, Lord. Won't it? If I can just involve Alex with Jason, help him to loosen up and relax with the boy, it would be so good for both of them.

Her prayers lately always revolved around the Caine family, in one way or another. She watched Jason pull the float through the water, making motorboat noises and sending ripples across the surface. Jason seemed to be keeping his word to her. There had been no incidents with matches. And he certainly smiled much more since Nugget had come into his life. Now if she could build a few bridges between him and his father, she'd feel she was accomplishing something.

Alex came out the back door, saw them in the pool, and hesitated for a moment before striding toward them. She suppressed a smile. Did Alex realize just how predictable he was? He treated swimming the way he did every other task in his life, approaching it with a determined work ethic. Of course, his swimming was therapy, but there was no reason why it couldn't also be fun.

He crossed the patio toward her, and a familiar tingle swept along her skin. *Keep your mind on the task,* she ordered herself.

"Hi." She looked up. He loomed above her on the pool deck, blocking the sun. "You have some company in the pool today. You don't mind, do you?"

"It's fine." To her surprise, he dropped his towel and sat down next to her. "I didn't know Kristie was coming."

Was there an undertone suggesting he should have known? He had told her to make arrangements about Jason's friends, she reminded herself.

"Gwen and I talked about it when she was leaving last night," she said. "She'd been looking for something to occupy her granddaughter now that school's out, and she thought swimming lessons would be perfect."

Alex's face relaxed as he watched the little carrottop try to balance a beach ball on her head. "She's a cute kid."

Her breath caught. That was how he'd looked with his friend Mitch the night before—off guard, as if he'd put away for a while the burden of being who he was. Why couldn't he seem to do that with his own son?

Maybe because it mattered too much. She thought again of those moments when he'd confided his concerns about the company. Alex was so intent on providing the proper lifestyle for his little boy that he didn't have time to play with him.

She remembered only too well the formal, intimidating presence of Alex's father. She'd been terrified of earning the elder Caine's disapproval on her visits. He certainly hadn't provided a role model for relaxed parenting. And like Jason, Alex had grown up without the softening presence of the mother who'd died when he was young. Maybe he just didn't know how to be closer to his son.

"Come on," she said, sliding into the water, cool after the heat radiating from the flagstones. She held out her hand in invitation. "Let's help the kids practice what they've learned."

For a moment she thought he'd follow her, but then he shook his head. "I have to get my laps in."

Of course he did. She tried not to feel disappointment. Changes wouldn't come in a day.

He walked toward the deep end, then paused, looking at her. "By the way, did the puppy serve his purpose?"

The sudden change of topic startled her, particularly since she'd been busy noticing the breadth of his shoulders. "What do you mean?"

"Your loneliness," he said. "Remember? You needed the puppy so you wouldn't be lonely in the cottage by yourself."

"Right." She couldn't stop a grin. "I'd have to say, he is a mixed blessing. He yipped until I gave up and let him spend the night on my bed."

He glanced toward the pen, where Nugget slept curled up on a rug. "It sounds as if that puppy knew how to get exactly what he wanted." He dove into the pool.

Maybe she could stand to cool off a bit herself. She submerged, then came up beside Jason's float, tilting her head back to let the water run off her hair.

"Why don't we practice your swimming," she suggested. Maybe when Alex saw what was going on, he'd be drawn in, just as he had their first time in the pool.

For the next few minutes she worked with the kids, careful to keep it fun. Kristie was more adventurous in the water than Jason, and her presence pushed him. He wouldn't want a girl, especially not a younger girl, to do something better than he did.

"Okay, let's practice blowing bubbles." She dipped her mouth under the water's surface, watching them closely.

Kristie put her whole face in, then came up sputtering. Jason, a little more cautious, screwed his eyes closed before trying.

"Good job!" Paula said when he'd come up again.

"Very good." Alex's voice, close behind her, made her jump. She'd been so intent on the children, she hadn't noticed his approach.

"I think putting your face in the water is the toughest part of learning to swim," she said, determined not to let him rattle her. "You two are doing great after just one lesson."

"I want to swim like you and my dad," Jason declared, bouncing on his toes. "I want to do regular strokes and go in the deep water and dive."

"You will." She pushed wet dark hair back from his eyes. "Give yourself a little time. Everything takes practice."

"Is Paula a good swimmer?" Alex gave her an innocent look. "I haven't seen her do anything but blow bubbles."

"I could probably give you a run for your money," she said.

"Is that a dare?"

"A race!" Kristie hopped up and down, clapping. "Have a race!"

"A race," Jason echoed. "Down to the end and back."

"Willing to put it to the test?" Alex's dark eyes held a challenge.

"You bet." She mentally measured the distance to the end of the pool. She might have overreached herself. "Jason, you be the starter."

Jason pulled himself to the pool deck and stood above them, raising his hand. "Ready, set, go!" he shouted.

Paula plunged into a shallow dive, surfacing with a strong, smooth stroke. It would take more than her best race to beat Alex. She churned through the water, glimpsing him from the corner of her eye. He didn't seem to be exerting himself at all.

They reached the end in nearly a dead heat, flipped and started back. *Outclassed,* she thought, watching him forge ahead of her effortlessly. She was definitely outclassed.

By the time she reached the end, he was standing there, smiling at her. She came up beside him.

"No fair," she gasped. "You're not even out of breath."

He seized her wet hands and pulled her upright. "Why is that unfair?" He grinned. "Because you lost? Maybe you'd like a handicap—say, three strokes?"

"More like five or six." She clung to his arm for a moment, getting her balance and her breath. Beyond Alex, she saw the children watching them. Kristie was grinning and clapping her hands. But

Jason—Jason wore an expression she couldn't interpret.

She glanced up at Alex, to find he watched her equally closely. His expression was just as difficult to read, but whatever it meant, it made her heart contract.

"I don't want to!" Jason ran out of the kitchen the next afternoon, slamming the door behind him.

Paula sighed and bent to ruffle the puppy's ears. "Looks as if we've lost our charm, Nugget."

He woofed softly, and she almost thought his eyes reflected her own disappointment.

She'd been so sure she was on the right track with Jason. Now she regretted that her daily reports to Maida had been so optimistic. She'd hit a roadblock with the boy, and she didn't know what to do about it.

Since she and Alex had raced, since she'd caught Jason watching them with that odd expression, the boy had been difficult—sullen, locked away from her as if their growing friendship had never been. He didn't even seem to take pleasure in the puppy. Everything she'd suggested, including time in the swimming pool, had been met the same way. *"I don't want to."*

She heard the front door open and close—*Alex*—and bent to put Nugget back in his pen. The puppy whimpered a bit, then began to chew on a toy.

I know how you feel, she told him silently. *I have to do something I don't want to do, too.*

But Alex had a right to know things weren't going well with his son, and she had a responsibility to tell him. She walked slowly to the swinging door and pushed through to the front of the house.

Alex stood in the wide center hallway, leafing through the mail she'd put on the heavy mahogany table. He glanced up at her step and smiled.

That smile had a regrettable tendency to take her breath away. "You're home from the plant early," she said, determined not to let him know his presence had an effect on her. "Is something wrong?"

"On the contrary." He dropped the envelopes back onto the table and came toward her. "Everything is remarkably good."

He looked lighter, as if a burden had been lifted from his shoulders.

"Really? What's happening?" She could use some good news to distract her from her worries about Jason and from her dread of telling Alex.

"I finished up my talks with Klemmer today."

Klemmer. It took her a moment to remember the representative of the Swiss firm—the man she'd nearly hit with a fly ball.

"And that's good?" she asked.

"More than good. He liked the plans I presented to him and recommended the firm to his company.

His boss will arrive next week to negotiate the deal.''

''Alex, that is good news.'' Without intending to, she reached out to him. He held both her hands in a firm, warm grip. For a moment they stood, hands clasped, very close together. Then she took a step back.

He released her immediately. ''Yes, it is good. Not settled yet, of course, but they wouldn't come all this way if they didn't like what we have to offer.''

''If it goes through—''

''It has to go through.'' His eyes darkened. ''It's our last chance. So everything has to go perfectly.''

She felt her nerves tense at his tone. Somehow she thought she was about to meet a hurdle. ''Which 'everything' did you have in mind?''

''Among other things, I have to entertain them. I thought a small dinner party a week from Friday. Nothing too large, no more than twenty people.''

She managed to keep herself from gasping. ''Twenty?''

''We'll use a caterer, of course.''

She could breathe again. No one expected her to cook for twenty.

''And we'll have the cleaners here an extra time,'' he went on. ''Come to the library, and I'll give you all the information you'll need.''

She followed him, trying to swallow her apprehension. She'd said she could do this. Now she had to live up to her word.

Alex riffled through a file before holding it out to her. Naturally he would have a file on entertaining. She thought again of her method of having guests, which usually consisted of ordered-in pizza. No, she was definitely out of her league now.

"That should have all the information you'll need, but if there's anything you don't understand, please ask me. I don't want any mistakes."

She held the folder, trying to think of a question to begin with, out of the many that crowded her mind. "Where are we going to seat that many people?"

He beckoned her to follow him again, and she trailed after him across the hall to the dining room.

"With the leaves in, the table seats sixteen. If there are more, the caterers will set up small tables. We'll talk about place cards and table arrangement when it gets a bit closer." He frowned at the heavy mahogany chairs, large enough to dwarf a normal human. "This room is tricky to arrange. I've always hated this furniture. The pieces we're making at the plant now are much more attractive."

She stared at him for a moment. "I don't understand. If you feel that way about it, why on earth don't you replace this...stuff?" She'd almost said *ugly stuff,* but caught herself in time.

"I couldn't do that." His response seemed almost automatic.

"Why not? It's your house."

His gaze lingered on the heavy oil portrait of his grandfather that hung over the dining room fireplace. "Sometimes I find that hard to believe."

His words were so quiet, he almost seemed to be speaking to himself. She wanted to argue, but instinctively she knew it wouldn't do any good. She'd been wrong. It wasn't his house, not in the way she understood those words. It was the Caine mansion, and right now Alex looked as if that were a heavy burden.

She frowned down at the folder. She had come into the hall intending to confide her worries about his son. But Alex already had his hands full. Maybe she should hold her tongue and try to handle this herself. Perhaps in another day Jason would regain his smile. *Coward,* a small voice said in her mind.

"I'll get started on this." She waved the folder.

Alex turned toward her, seeming to shake off the clouds that surrounded him. "Thank you." He reached out to clasp her hand again. The warmth of his grip shimmered along her skin.

"For what? It's my job." It was hard to sound casual when her heart clenched at his closeness.

"For being here. For helping me." His fingers moved caressingly along the back of her hand. "I'm glad you're back."

She wasn't sure she actually walked back to the kitchen. It felt much more like floating. She didn't want to look too closely at what she was feeling, because that might make it vanish, like mist on the mountain burned off by the sun.

Clutching the folder, she pushed through the door into the kitchen—and came to a halt. Nugget slept in his pen. The sauce she'd started for dinner simmered on the stove. But Aunt Maida's recipe box lay in the middle of the floor, broken into pieces.

Alex put another weight into place on the machine and slid onto the seat, hooking his legs behind the padded bar. Maybe if he pushed his body hard enough, he could keep his emotions at bay.

Ten repetitions later, he knew it wasn't working. His injured leg complained at the added weight, but that wasn't what bothered him.

Paula had caught him off guard. He'd told himself he had neither the time nor the inclination to get involved with her. He'd promised her that what happened the last time she was here wouldn't happen again. But each time he was near her, it became more difficult to keep that promise.

He forced himself into another set of reps, gritting his teeth against the pain. Brett would say Alex was pushing too hard. But Brett, newly married to the physician's assistant in his office, wasn't fighting a wave of longing for something he'd never have. He tried to remember feeling this way for his wife, but he couldn't. This was something new.

Is it so impossible? The treacherous question slid into his mind and refused to be dislodged. He'd convinced himself that happily-ever-after didn't exist, but his closest friends seemed to have found it.

He concentrated on his exercises, trying to bury the thought. It refused to be buried.

"Alex?"

The weights clanged down as he swung toward the sound. He hadn't heard Paula come in, but there she was, looking around the exercise room his friends had created in the old conservatory.

"I'm sorry. I shouldn't interrupt you when you're working out." She looked as if she wanted to back right out the door.

"Don't worry about it." He slid off the machine, willing his knee not to waver at the punishment he'd been dealing it. He grabbed a towel, feeling a wave of embarrassment at being caught this way. "I was about done anyway."

"I… There's something I need to talk with you about."

Whatever it was, she clearly didn't want to bring it up. He could almost see the reluctance surrounding her.

"All right." He tossed the towel over the machine. "If it's something about the party, we can go over the notes together." He was astounded at the amount of pleasure generated by that thought. Paula hadn't just caught him off guard—she'd gotten under his skin.

"No, it's not the party. It's this—"

She held something out to him. Frowning, he crossed the room to her.

"That's Maida's recipe box, isn't it? What happened to it?" The wooden box that always sat on the counter next to the stove had been broken into several pieces.

"I'm afraid Jason broke it."

Her gravity seemed all out of proportion to the event. He took the pieces from her, turning them over in his hands. "I'd say, get a new box, but I know Maida prized this one." He smiled at her. "Because you gave it to her, as I recall. I think it can be fixed."

"That's not the point." She looked at the box, then up at him. "When I said Jason broke it, I didn't mean it was an accident. He broke it on purpose."

For a long moment he could only stare at her. Then anger kicked in. "What are you talking about? Why on earth would you think that?"

"I don't think it, I know it."

There was no matching anger in her face, only sorrow.

"Alex, I'm sorry. I feel like a talebearer, but I didn't think I should handle this on my own. Jason was angry—he's been angry all day. And he broke the box deliberately. He told me.''

He wanted to say he didn't believe it, but he couldn't. "Why? Why was he angry?''

She took an audible breath. "He wouldn't tell me, but I think I know." Peachy color flooded her cheeks. "He was watching us yesterday, in the pool. When we were…when we were close to each other. I think it bothered him. He's been angry ever since.''

"I can't accept that." The words were out before he thought about it. "You must be wrong, about all of this. My son doesn't behave that way.''

A spark of anger lit her eyes at that. "Why? Because he's a Caine? Because Caines don't have normal human feelings?''

Whatever softness he'd felt toward her was wiped from the slate now. He leaned toward her. "I know my son better than you do. He's been taught what appropriate behavior is.''

"Appropriate—Alex, he's a little boy, and he's hurting." Her voice rose, impassioned. "For some reason, he was bothered by seeing us together. I don't know why, but I know we can't ignore it.''

"I don't intend to ignore it." His grip tightened on the pieces of the box, but he kept his voice cool and controlled. "Jason is my responsibility, not yours. I'll take care of the situation, if it exists. I don't care to discuss it with you any further.''

She jerked back as if he'd struck her. "Fine."
She was as pale now as she'd been flushed earlier.
"I'd nearly forgotten. I'm just the housekeeper.
You handle it."

She whirled and nearly ran out of the room.

Chapter Eight

This picnic was going to be no fun at all, Paula decided as she sat next to Alex in the car. At least, not if her enjoyment depended on the status of her relationship with Alex.

She glanced across at him, but if he felt her gaze, Alex didn't respond. Meanwhile, Jason moped in the back seat.

No fun at all.

"I'll bet lots of your friends will be at the picnic," she told Jason, trying to sound cheerful. After all, somebody had to.

"I wanted to bring Nugget." His lower lip came out in a pout. "He'd like a picnic."

Alex had flatly refused to bring the puppy, with good reason.

"Don't you think a picnic would be too exciting

for a puppy?" she asked. "I know you'll enjoy it, but Nugget is still just a baby. He might be frightened of all the noise and people."

Jason clearly hadn't considered that. His gaze met hers in the rearview mirror. "But he'd be with me. He wouldn't be scared if he was with me. Besides, there'd be lots of good stuff to eat."

"For people, not for dogs," Alex pointed out. "Remember what the vet told Paula. Only puppy food is good for puppies."

"That's right." She welcomed the opportunity to agree with Alex on something, after the battle royal they'd had several days earlier. "You wouldn't want him to get sick."

"I guess." Jason acted reluctant to give up his grievance. "Can I give him a treat when we get home?"

"Sure." She smiled at him in the mirror, and after a moment got a hint of a smile in return.

At least her relationship with Jason had settled down. He wasn't quite as open as he'd been, but now he played with the puppy and went back in the pool. Whatever had been bothering him, whatever had led to his breaking the recipe box, he seemed to have gotten control of his feelings. Like his father, Jason always had to be in control.

Control was certainly the defining word when it came to the Caine men. Alex had been rigidly polite to her since their quarrel. Maybe if she apologized for her outburst, things would get back to normal.

No, she couldn't do that. She probably hadn't been very tactful, but she'd said what needed to be said, and there was no one else to do that.

Alex stopped the car at the bottom of the steep lane, waiting while a cluster of tourists crossed the street, heading for the parking lot along the river. One woman carried a handmade quilt encased in a plastic bag over her arm, while another juggled three bags from Ellie Wayne's gift shop.

"Now you see why we have the picnic in the evening." Alex nodded toward the tourists. "The shops will close soon. No one would want to risk losing business during the tourist season."

It was the first conversational thing he'd said to her since their argument. Maybe that meant he was ready to put the disagreement behind them.

"I guess if you run a shop like Ellie's, you probably have to make money while you can."

He nodded. "There's not much market for hand-made baskets and dried flowers in the middle of winter." He shot a sideways glance at her that was almost a smile, and the tension inside her began to ease. "Bedford Creek tends to hibernate in the off-season."

He turned up the steep street that led to Grace Church. From the Caine mansion, the church steeple was clearly visible across the narrow valley.

Maida had told her that an earlier Caine had donated the land for the church and even paid for the steeple, so he could have a good view of it from his windows. It took a bit longer to drive there, down and up the narrow, hilly streets, than it would take a sparrow to fly.

Bedford Creek seemed crammed into its tight valley, spreading upward from the river because there was no other place for it to go. Above the town the mountain ridge, dark with hemlocks, cut off the sky.

Paula looked out at narrow clapboard houses whose colorful window boxes were filled with pansies and ageratum. Bedford Creek dressed in its finest for the tourists who came to enjoy the mountain scenery and buy at the quilt store, the basket shop, the bakery, the candlemaker's. In addition to Alex's factory, tourism was the town's only source of income. Could it get by on that if the factory failed? She doubted it. No wonder Alex felt such a burden.

He pulled into the church parking lot. "Looks as if we'll have a good turnout." His unexpected smile erased the last vestige of tension from their quarrel. "Enjoy yourself, Paula. You're not here as part of your job, remember."

She smiled back, her spirits lifting. She just might enjoy herself at that.

Tables had been set up under the trees on the park-like grounds surrounding the church. To her relief, she saw some faces that were familiar from other years, other visits.

Alex took the picnic basket she was holding, then leaned close. "Don't let them overwhelm you," he murmured. "They're good at that."

She nodded, not trusting her voice. She was in danger of being overwhelmed, all right, but not by friendly church members.

But by the time she started through the buffet line, she wasn't so sure. She'd already given updates on Maida's condition to at least a dozen people and had promised to deliver get-well wishes. She tried to remember names, knowing her aunt would want to know who'd asked about her, but they began to blur in her mind.

As she reached for a scoop of fruit salad, Gwen bustled up to her, bringing the line to a halt. "Now, Paula, I have several quarts of homemade soup in the car to give you. Don't get away without it."

Paula looked at her blankly. Why was Gwen giving her soup? Was it something Maida had ordered and forgotten to tell her about?

"It'll do for lunches, and as soon as Maida comes home, we'll start bringing in suppers, too," the woman went on. "You'll have your hands full, running that big house and looking after Maida."

"You don't have to do that," Paula began, but Gwen went on as if she hadn't spoken.

"Probably I should line up people to stay with

Maida right at first. Yes, that would be best. I'll let you know when I have a schedule set up.''

''I don't need any help,'' Paula protested, but it was too late. Gwen had bustled away again, looking like a busy little brown wren on her self-appointed errand.

''You may as well let them help.'' The amused voice came from behind her, and she turned to find that Pastor Richie was the next person in line. The rotund, white-haired man smiled with sympathy. ''I know Gwen can be overbearing, but everyone wants to help.''

''But...'' *I want to do it myself.* That would certainly sound ungracious, but it was what she felt. ''The doctor wants Aunt Maida to go into rehab, so she won't be home for a couple of weeks at least. And I'm sure I can handle things, even when Maida comes home.''

''Of course you can, but that's not the point, is it?''

She looked at him blankly. If that wasn't the point, what was?

Pastor Richie helped himself to a heaping spoonful of scalloped potatoes, then sighed. ''I might be able to lose weight, if I could bear to turn down one dish. But then someone's feelings might be hurt.''

It took a moment to realize what he was saying.

"You mean people's feelings will be hurt if I don't let them help."

He nodded, and his bright blue eyes were intent. "That's true, of course. People here love Maida, so they're quite ready to love you, sort of by extension. But it's more than that. If you don't let them help, you might do them harm."

"Do them harm?" she echoed. Why on earth would her being independent harm anyone else?

"People need to be of service to others," he said. He added a dollop of cranberry salad to an already overflowing plate. "It's a spiritual blessing, you see. You wouldn't want to deprive anyone of a spiritual blessing, would you?"

"No...no, of course not." Like Aunt Maida, the pastor clearly saw the world in spiritual terms.

He beamed. "Then you'll let them help. You can always tell yourself it's for Maida, not for you, if that makes you feel better."

She looked at him with surprise and respect. How had he known that was what she'd do? And what else did his wise eyes see when they looked at her?

"Paula, over here." She glanced toward the voice, to discover Mitch Donovan, seated with a group at one of the folding tables, waving at her to join them.

It wasn't until she reached them that she realized Alex was there. She hesitated, not sure whether he'd consider this appropriate. He'd told her she wasn't on duty at the picnic. Did that mean he'd prefer not to socialize with her?

He answered that by pulling out the chair next to him. "Join us, please."

She sat, very aware of his movements as he adjusted her chair and handed her a napkin. Would she ever get over this hyper-awareness when it came to Alex Caine?

"I think you know some of these people. Mitch, of course, and Brett."

Paula nodded to Brett. If she'd thought about it, she'd have realized Alex would be sitting with these two men. They'd long been his closest friends.

"This is Mitch's wife, Anne."

A beautiful, dark-haired woman looked up from the toddler on her lap and held out her hand. "Welcome to Bedford Creek, Paula."

"And you know Brett's wife, Rebecca. She's the physician's assistant at the clinic now."

"I'll see you often once your aunt is discharged from the hospital." Rebecca had a warm, sunny smile to match her auburn hair and peaches-and-cream complexion. "You'll be bringing her to the clinic for her checkups, I'm sure."

Paula nodded, a little overwhelmed with all this friendliness. They acted as if she were Alex's guest, instead of his housekeeper.

Anne seemed to sense her discomfort. She turned

the conversation to the current tourist season, urging Mitch to tell a story about the enterprising young man who'd tried to set up a souvenir shop in the town's park.

With the focus off her and the talk bouncing comfortably around the table, Paula tried to sort them all out. Anne was an attorney, she remembered hearing, and the toddler on her lap was adopted. Rebecca was Gwen's daughter, little Kristie's aunt, and she'd inherited her mother's warmth.

Paula noticed something else after she'd listened to them for a few minutes. With these people, Alex was at ease. With everyone else, as far as she'd been able to observe, the Caine shield stayed in place, marking the boundary between him and the rest of the world. But with Brett and Mitch, and perhaps with their wives, he was himself.

She saw his firm mouth relax, his eyes crinkle with laughter, and her heart seemed to cramp. If he ever reached that point with her...but there was no sense imagining something that would never happen.

Anne leaned across to her under cover of the general conversation. "That's our foster son, Davey, kicking the soccer ball with Jason and Kristie."

The lanky preteen towered over the smaller children, but he kicked the ball gently enough so that Jason had a shot at it. "He seems like a very nice boy."

Anne smiled with maternal pride. "He's come a long way, believe me. Mitch is terrific with him."

"I imagine you have something to do with it, too."

"I try." She stroked the soft curls of the sleepy toddler on her lap. "How are you doing with Jason? I know from Maida he can be a little difficult."

The urge to confide her concerns to a sympathetic ear was strong, but she resisted it. She didn't have the right to say anything about Jason, even to someone who was Alex's friend.

"I think we're getting along pretty well. I'm sure he misses Maida, though." Surely it was all right to say that much.

"Maida's been like a grandmother to that child." Anne seemed to read between the lines. She touched Paula's hand lightly. "Jason's had too many losses in his young life. And it can't be easy living up to the Caine name."

It was so near what she herself thought that she had to clench her teeth to keep from blurting something out.

Anne smiled. "If you ever need someone to talk to, just give me a call."

"Thanks." She had the sense that, improbable as it might seem, she'd made a friend. "I'll do that."

Nobody seemed able to make him as angry as Paula could with just a word. Alex smiled wryly as he walked slowly across the patio. Perhaps he needed to remind himself that the rest of the world wouldn't treat him with the deference most people in Bedford Creek did. Certainly Paula didn't. He suspected only her desire to keep her job had prevented her from saying even more than she had.

She seemed, without being aware of it, to have joined the select group that actually looked at him as just another human being. Certainly Brett and Mitch knew his weaknesses as well as he did himself, and didn't hesitate to call him to order if they felt he needed it. Now Paula had come on board, and he didn't know how to handle that.

He'd watched her at the picnic. He'd seen her fitting into his town, fitting into his life, as if she belonged here.

Nonsense. He tried to reject that idea out of hand. Paula worked for him. She neither wanted nor would welcome anything else.

She was the only woman willing to defy him. Maybe she was also the only woman who could really accept him.

That was a dangerous thought. He wasn't ready to take that kind of risk again. He—

A cry echoed through the gathering dusk, startling him. Was it a bird of some sort? Then it came again, and he knew instinctively what he'd heard. *Paula!* He began to run toward the garage, toward that panicked cry.

His heart thudded in his ears as he rounded the building. She was in trouble, she was hurt, she—

An errant flame, stirred by the breeze, licked upward from the brush the lawn service had been burning earlier. He'd have something to say to them about that. Then he saw Paula's face, and her expression banished every other thought from his mind.

She was terrified. She stood backed against the garage wall, clutching the puppy in her arms. She looked unable to move, and she stared, eyes wide and frightened, into the flames.

"Paula!" He grasped her arm, pulling her away from the fire. Another dry branch caught, flaring up. He couldn't stop the images that flooded his mind—the flames rushing toward them, working frantically to free Paula from the seat, knowing that at any moment it could be too late...

That must be what Paula saw, too.

"It's all right." He turned her toward him, frightened at her reaction, and held her face between his hands. His heart still pounded, but he willed his voice to stay calm. "Paula, look at me, not the fire. It's all right, do you hear me? You're safe."

For several seconds she didn't respond, as if she couldn't hear him. Then, finally, she blinked. The terror was still in her eyes, but she focused on his face.

"You're safe," he said, longing to pull her into

his arms and not daring to. "Can you stay right here while I get the hose and put that out?"

She swallowed, the muscles in her throat working. Then she nodded. The puppy wiggled and yelped, but she gripped it tighter.

"Good." His voice nearly betrayed him, but he wouldn't let it. He couldn't let her know how shaken he was by her reaction. "I'll just be a minute."

He let go of her tentatively. She took a gasping breath, then nodded again.

Alex hurried around the garage, grabbed the coiled hose and twisted the tap on. He ran back to Paula, ignoring the throbbing in his injured leg, and aimed the nozzle at the flames. Moments later, only a blackened circle marred the grass.

He brushed his hands on his pant legs as he went back to her. "The lawn service should never have left that brush pile behind the garages." Maybe talking would erase the shock from her face. "It's out now, and no harm done."

That had to be the stupidest remark he'd ever made. He desperately wanted the tension to be over. He wanted them both to smile and walk away.

But that couldn't happen, not now. This was one time when keeping a stiff upper lip and smiling through the pain wouldn't cut it. He put his arm around her gently and felt her tremble.

"Come on." He led her a step. "Let's go in the house. We need to talk."

She tried to pull away, embarrassment flooding her face. "No, I...I don't need to do that. I'm fine." Her voice seemed to gain strength as she spoke.

A few days ago he'd have accepted that. He'd have used it for an excuse to back away from a conversation that had to be painful for both of them. Now he couldn't. Paula's return had changed things. Her agony forced its way beneath his protective barrier, wrenching his heart. Pretending everything was all right was no longer an option.

He caught her hand, holding it firmly. "You're not fine, and we need to talk." He brushed his thumb over her knuckles, as gently as if she were a child.

She looked away from him. "There's nothing to talk about. I just have this stupid fear of fire."

"I can see that. And we both know why."

"I was chasing Nugget," she said, ignoring the reference to the accident. "When the flames flared up in front of me, I just panicked for a moment."

"Paula—"

"That's all it was." She tried to pull away.

He tightened his grasp on her hand. She was doing what he always did—tamping down the pain, ignoring it, ignoring anyone who brought it up. He was just beginning to realize how futile that was.

"I'm not satisfied with that explanation. You

might get away with it with anyone else, but not me.''

She looked at him then, and he read the pain in her eyes so clearly.

''I don't...''

He shook his head. ''Don't even try, because I'm the one person in the world you can't fool on this subject. I was there, remember?'' He never talked about the crash. He was going to. ''Like it or not, we shared something terrifying and lived to tell about it.''

Somehow those didn't seem to be the right words.

''No, not 'tell about it,''' he amended. ''You haven't been talking about it, I'm sure of that. And maybe you need to.''

''Talking won't make it go away.''

''Nothing will make it go away, but we have to deal with it.'' Her pain was forcing him inch by painful inch from behind his own protective barricade. ''I've got scars on the outside from the crash. But you—you're carrying your scars inside. And like it or not, we're going to talk about this.''

Chapter Nine

Paula wanted to argue, to insist that she was all right, but she couldn't. Her stomach still churned, and the metallic taste of fear lingered in her mouth. She wasn't all right, and both of them knew it.

She let Alex pilot her into the house. He seemed to hesitate for a moment, as if trying to decide where to go, then led her into the sunroom that adjoined the kitchen.

The gathering dusk seeped into the room through the wall of windows, chilling her. Alex switched on a table lamp, and its golden glow banished the darkness.

"Sit down here." He pushed her gently onto the chintz sofa, then ran his hands down her arms. "You're cold. I'm going to make a cup of Maida's herbal tea for you." He shoved a hassock under her feet. "I'll just be a minute. Do you want me to take the dog?"

"No." The word was out before she had a chance to think about it. She stroked Nugget's soft fur, taking comfort from his warmth. "I'll keep him with me. You don't need to—"

But he was gone. She leaned back against the overstuffed cushions. The couch gave under her, cradling her body, offering further comfort. Maybe that was what she needed. Her legs still trembled, as if she'd run a marathon. She'd just relax a minute; then she could assure Alex she was fine and leave.

The small room, so out of place amid the formality of the rest of the mansion, welcomed her. Its soft colors were feminine and restful, and the dried flower arrangements and faded chintzes would have been appropriate in her parents' house. It hardly seemed possible that the same person who'd chosen mahogany bedroom suites suitable for Buckingham Palace had decorated this cozy haven.

She heard Alex's steps in the kitchen, their faint unevenness the only hint of his injured leg. Then he was back. He put a white pottery mug in her hands, sat down next to her and moved the sleeping puppy from her lap to a spot between them.

"Drink that. Maida's chamomile tea is guaranteed to make any trouble better."

She remembered all the times she'd sat across

from Maida at the kitchen table, drinking her aunt's special brew, talking about anything and everything. Steam curled from the pale liquid, and she sipped cautiously.

Warmth suffused her, calming the quaking inside. Her muscles relaxed as the tension seeped away, leaving her limp and exhausted. As the last shadow of the nightmare vanished, she looked across at Alex, seeing him with a clarity she'd never before experienced.

He leaned back, his long fingers absently stroking the sleeping puppy. He seemed perfectly at ease, as if willing to wait all night, if need be, for her. Even the lines around his firm mouth had relaxed, erasing the formal reserve he normally projected. He was watching the puppy, and his dark lashes hid his eyes from her. His skin, tanned from his hours in the pool, contrasted with the white knit shirt he'd worn to the picnic.

He looked up suddenly, and their eyes met. Awareness of him shimmered along her skin and took her breath away.

"Better now?" His dark gaze probed.

"Yes." Her heartbeat accelerated, the tension returning. He was going to push her for answers, and she wouldn't be able to withstand him. He'd drag her weakness out into the light for both of them to see.

"This is a nice room, isn't it?" He ran his hand along the rose chintz arm of the sofa.

She blinked, surprised. That certainly wasn't the question she'd expected. He was giving her time, she realized. The hard questions still lurked, held in abeyance until he thought she could handle them.

She took another swallow of the tea. "It's a cozy room." She tried to smile, suspecting the result didn't look very convincing. "I've always thought this spot doesn't match the rest of the mansion."

"That's because my mother decorated it. My father insisted the rest of the house be left in its turn-of-the-century grandeur, but this room was hers." He touched the faded blossoms of a dried flower arrangement, his long fingers gentle. "She loved flowers. That's one of the few things I remember about her—the scent of flowers."

His words reached out and clutched her heart. Alex was exposing feelings he usually kept hidden. Maybe he did it because that was what he expected from her. He'd consider that fair. She might deplore Alex's arrogance, but she'd never doubted his fairness.

"I'm sorry." Her throat tightened. "It must have been hard, not having a mother when you were growing up." Her thoughts flickered to her mother, then Aunt Maida—two very different female influences in her life.

"Now my son is going through the same thing."

The lines around his eyes deepened. "The Caine family doesn't seem destined for 'happily every after.'"

"Jason will be fine." She answered the doubt under his words. "He just needs..." She stopped, not sure she should go on.

"What do you think Jason needs?" The usual defensive note was missing from his voice. He asked as if he really wanted an answer.

He needs the same thing you do. "He needs to open up to someone." She took a breath and waited—for an explosion, for him to freeze her out or give her that superior look that said her opinion wasn't worth hearing. For him to retort immediately that his son was fine, as he always did.

Instead, he put his hand over hers. "Isn't that what you need, Paula?"

There it was—the question he'd been waiting to ask, the question she knew she had to answer. "I don't know." The words didn't want to come out, but she forced them out, anyway. "Maybe I need courage. Maybe I'm really a coward, letting myself panic over a simple thing like fire." Her mind flickered to Jason and the matches. But he had been asleep for hours. He couldn't have had any thing to do with this.

"The accident—"

She swept on, the words suddenly rushing out now that she'd started. "You don't know, do you?

I don't even remember the accident! It's wiped right out of my mind. So why should I have this stupid panic when I see flames? It doesn't make any sense.''

"You don't remember anything about the accident?"

"Nothing." Her mouth twisted. "My family insists that's lucky. Maybe they're right."

He stroked her hand, in much the same way he'd stroked the sleeping puppy. "I'm not so sure. Maybe your conscious mind doesn't remember, but something inside you does."

She hadn't thought of it that way, but, of course, he was right. Something in her remembered and was terrified. "I feel like it's hiding there, in my mind." She took a shaky breath. "Just waiting to jump out and grab me."

"I'm sorry I didn't know." His fingers wrapped around hers. "I asked Maida how you were so many times, but she didn't tell me this."

"It makes me feel like a failure." The words tasted bitter. "I try to be strong, but in this…" *But I'm not.* She choked, and couldn't go on. She'd run out of steam, with her pitiful weakness laid out for both of them to see.

Alex took her hand and held it between his palms. His warmth and strength seemed to flow along her skin. "Paula, that's nonsense. You must know it. Nobody can go through what we went through and not have scars. Believe me. Do you think I don't have nightmares about the crash?''

She blinked rapidly to hold back hot tears. ''You're functioning. You don't let your fears paralyze you.''

''Maybe not, but everyone is different. You take any group of people and put them in a life-threatening situation, and each one of them will respond in a unique way.'' His hands tightened on hers. ''Believe me, I know. I've been through it twice.''

''Twice?'' For a moment she didn't know what he was talking about, but then half-forgotten words came back to her. ''I remember.'' She shook her head. ''A little, anyway. I overheard Aunt Maida talking to someone about you. But then when she saw I was there, she changed the subject.''

''She probably didn't want you to think about imitating our stupidity.''

'''Our'?''

''Brett's, Mitch's and mine. We came close to wiping ourselves off the planet on a class camping trip our senior year in high school.''

His words were light, but the rigidity of his jaw muscles belied that. He was trying to help by telling her this, but it was costing him.

''What happened?''

''A flash flood. You know how fast the streams can go up when we've had heavy rain.''

She nodded, unable to suppress a shiver. The valley was so narrow, there was no place for the water to go. "You were trapped, weren't you?"

"We were stupid. Or maybe just too immature to be let out alone. Each group in our class was supposed to find its way through the woods with a compass and a map. Instead, we got lost and ended up in an abandoned quarry with the water rising around us."

His voice sounded perfectly calm, but his hand clenched hers so tightly it hurt.

"You could have died." Just as they both could have died that rainy night at the airfield.

He gave a tight nod. "I slipped into the water. If Mitch hadn't grabbed me, within minutes I'd have been just a memory."

"But you did get out, all three of you." If he was trying to make her feel better about her pitiful weakness, he hadn't succeeded. "You survived that. You survived the plane crash. You didn't let either of those things keep you from moving on." If he did have nightmares, as he claimed, he'd beaten them into submission.

He seemed to realize how tightly he gripped her hand, and loosened his hold with a small, apologetic smile. But he didn't let go.

"I'm not making my point very well. All of us were affected by what happened. In the long run it made us stronger, but at the time it wasn't easy. For you, it's flames. For me, it's rain. I can't hear rain on the roof without breaking out in a cold sweat.'' He shrugged. "Other people didn't help after the accident. They either acted as if we were heroes for getting out or stupid for getting into the situation in the first place.''

That brought her startled gaze up to his face. "No one would blame you for an accident.''

"No?'' Something faintly mocking appeared in his eyes. "You don't remember my father very well if you think that.''

Yes, she remembered that rigid autocrat. "What did he say to you?''

"Just the usual sort of thing.'' His tone was light, but pain threaded through it, sharp and hard. "That I'd failed. I hadn't lived up to my responsibilities. I should have gotten excused from the trip, should have had better sense than to go in the quarry. My position as his heir was too important to risk on childish adventures.''

His words pierced her heart. Alex wasn't invulnerable, after all. He might try to convince himself that it didn't matter, but his father's harshness had damaged him. She actually found herself feeling pity for the man who had everything.

And she felt something else, too. Something she'd been trying to deny but couldn't any longer, even if she could never say it aloud.

She was still in love with him.

* * *

Alex heard the pain in his admission, and it shocked him. What was he doing? He was saying things to Paula that he'd never said to anyone, not his closest friends, not even his wife. The lessons he'd learned early had been too deeply ingrained. A Caine didn't feel weakness. And if he did, he certainly never admitted it.

Paula was different. Karin had bought into the whole Caine mystique, but Paula never did. She saw him as a person, not just the Caine heir. He wanted to tell Paula the things he'd kept hidden in his very soul. He wanted to give in to that fierce attraction he felt every time he was near her. He wanted to stop thinking about what he should do or shouldn't do, and follow his instincts. For once in his life, he wanted to put his intellectual side on hold and just feel. Maybe, for the first time, he'd found someone with whom he could let down all the barriers.

She was looking at him with a mixture of emotions in her clear-as-glass green eyes—sympathy, tenderness, caring. Those feelings drew him in. They pulled him closer and closer to her. Close enough that he could feel the warmth that emanated from her skin. Close enough that he could smell the fresh, flowery scent she wore. Close enough that their lips could meet...

For once he wouldn't stop and analyze this. His hand moved, almost without volition, and he stroked her smooth cheek. He brushed back a strand of golden hair, and it clung to his fingers as if to pull him even closer.

Her breath went out in a soft sigh, moving across his cheek. He turned her face toward him, overwhelmed with a rush of longing and tenderness. His lips found hers.

She was soft, so soft. She moved closer, nestling into his arms as if this was the most natural thing in the world. The kiss deepened, saying all the things he couldn't find words for.

Finally she drew away. "Alex." She sighed his name, her cheek warm against his.

His breath came out unevenly. "That's been a long time coming."

She pulled back, looking into his eyes, and her hand rested over his heart. "Not for me."

He looked questioningly at her.

"That's another thing Aunt Maida didn't tell you. What happened then, when I was here before," she paused, as if preparing herself for something. "I didn't remember any of it. Working here, being Jason's nanny—it was all wiped out. I know my parents wanted me treated at the bigger hospital in Baltimore, but I didn't remember going back. My memories started again in the hospital there. I didn't remember that summer until Aunt Maida asked me to come back. And it was as if a door fell open in my mind, and there it was."

He frowned, trying to assimilate her words. "You mean, all this time, you hadn't remembered anything from that summer?"

She shook her head. "I didn't remember. I still don't remember the actual crash—" She broke off sharply.

Her eyes widened, and the hand that had rested over his heart gripped his shirt.

"Paula, what is it?" She'd turned sheet-white. "What's wrong?"

"The...the a-accident," she stammered. "I didn't remember it. But now—" She stopped again, her pupils dilating.

"Paula." He gripped her arms. "You've remembered. Is that it?" Something—maybe that kiss, echoing the one two years ago, or maybe talking openly about the accident at last must have brought it back.

She couldn't seem to answer. Then she nodded. Her eyes focused on the past, dark with pain.

He knew what she was seeing. He'd seen it often enough himself. The ground rushing toward them, the grinding crash, the crumpled seats and panicked passengers. The flames.

"Paula, it's all right." She didn't respond. He pulled her against him, wrapping his arms around her as if that would protect her from the images in her mind. "It's all right. It's over. You don't have to think about it any more."

"I don't want to." Her voice choked with tears. "I don't want to! All this time I couldn't, and now I can't get the pictures out of my head."

"I know, I know." He stroked her hair, and her pain surrounded his heart. "But it's a long time ago."

"Not for me!" She sounded almost angry, but her hands clung tightly and her voice was muffled against his chest. "It's right now."

He understood then. Time had blurred his memories of the crash. Bad as they were, the jagged edges had been smoothed away, eased by layers of other events, happier memories.

But not for Paula. Paula was experiencing it now as he'd experienced it those first few days in the hospital, when he couldn't close his eyes without seeing it all again.

He cradled her against him, rocking her as gently. Her hot tears soaked into his shirt. "Hush, it's all right." They were the words he'd wanted to hear someone say to him. "It was terrifying, but you're all right. There's nothing to fear."

Her pain pierced his control. *Lord, help her.* He so seldom asked God's help for himself, thinking that surely God expected him to handle his own responsibilities. But help for Paula was different. *Give her peace, Lord. Please. She's in such pain.*

All he could do was hold her, tightly, as if he could absorb the pain. He let her cry, and her sobs ripped through him, shaking him in ways he didn't begin to understand.

One thing was clear, though. His feelings for Paula couldn't be tidied away as convenient or unsuitable. Like it or not, she roused emotion in him that he wasn't prepared to handle.

Why not? Why couldn't he and Paula, like any other two people, find a way to build something together? He'd told himself he didn't believe in happy endings. Nothing in his experience had led him to think one could exist for him. But maybe, with Paula, things could be different.

They didn't have to be just employer and employee. They didn't have to fall into the roles life had assigned them. Paula was an intelligent, giving, lovely woman, not the child who'd looked at him with hero worship in her eyes. They could start again, put the mistakes of the past behind them, and begin as equals.

Gradually her sobs trailed off. The death grip she'd had on his shirt relaxed. Next, he thought, she'd become embarrassed. Independent Paula never wanted to admit that she'd shown what she'd call weakness.

She eased back, still in the circle of his arms, and rubbed her eyes. "I'm sorry."

He had to smile at the predictability of the words. "Don't be sorry. You've relived a terrible experience. Of course you cried—anyone would."

"I didn't just cry." She touched his wet shirt. "I bawled like a baby. You must be ready to run for cover."

"Not yet." His heart lifted. She was past the worst of it. *Thank you, God.*

"Right." She mopped her eyes with her sleeve. "Men hate it when women cry."

"Depends on the man." He touched her cheek lightly, brushing away the tear that sparkled there. "And the woman."

He felt the warmth rise in her cheeks at his words, and it made him want to kiss her again.

"I don't like behaving like a baby," she said stubbornly. "Especially—" The words broke off, and her gaze evaded his.

"Especially in front of me? Am I that much of an ogre?" He needed to make her smile again.

"No." A smile trembled on her lips. "Not an ogre. But you are my boss, remember?"

"That doesn't mean I can't also be..." He shouldn't push it, not when she was so fragile. He had to smile at the thought of her probable reaction if he called her "fragile" aloud. "A friend," he finished. "Haven't we always been friends?"

The word seemed to reassure her, and he sensed some of the tension leave her.

"A friend," she agreed. "You've gone above and beyond the call of friendship tonight."

"I've been there," he reminded her. "I know what it feels like."

She nodded. Her eyes narrowed, as if she approached the memory again, very cautiously. "I always wondered about it, even when I tried not to. What it was like, how I got out."

"Now you know." He moved a little away from her. "It will be easier now. You remember, so you can let the memories start to fade."

She frowned. "Is that what yours have done?"

"Most of the time." He had to be honest with her. "Sometimes the thoughts bother me, but most of the time, even if something reminds me, I can put it aside and go on."

How long? he wondered. How long until he could stop being the supportive friend and move to being the interested male?

Her forehead was wrinkled, her gaze focused on the past. "Put it aside," she echoed. "Not hear it, not see it." She shivered. "Not smell it. That's the worst. Maybe that's why I get so panicked around fire. I smell it, and I want to run. But I can't. I'm trapped…"

Her eyes widened as she stared at him. "That's true, isn't it? I was trapped."

Reluctantly he nodded. He didn't want her to think about that, but it wasn't in him to lie to her. "You were trapped."

"The flames. I couldn't get the belt loose. I couldn't move."

She was reliving it again; he could see that. He reached for her, longing to wipe the memories away, and knowing he couldn't.

"But you did. We both got out."

She shook her head as if trying to shake the image away. "I was trapped." She focused on him suddenly. "You got me out. I remember now. You came—you got me out of the belt."

"Paula..." What could he say? That he didn't want her to go there?

"You dragged me to the hole in the cabin." A shudder passed through her. "People were crying. You took my hands and lowered me out of the plane. You told me to get away."

"Everyone got out," he reminded her. "It could have been so much worse. Everyone got out alive."

"But you saved me." She reached toward him. "You saved me."

He realized what was happening, and the hope he'd felt moments before turned to ashes. Paula wasn't looking at him like the woman who'd returned his kisses. She was looking at him like a starry-eyed, hero-worshipping child.

He drew back, fighting the fierce disappointment that swept through him. He couldn't do it. He couldn't pursue a relationship with Paula

when she thought of him as some kind of a hero.
Not when he was only too aware of how often he
failed to measure up. They couldn't build anything on that.

Chapter Ten

❧

"Come on, Jason. You can do it." Paula waved her mitt. "Throw it right in here."

Jason looked doubtful, but he pitched the baseball. His expression turned to astonishment when the throw made it across the makeshift plate and thunked into Paula's mitt.

Smiling, she stepped back and motioned one of the other peewee baseball players to take her place. When she'd learned the group of youngest kids from the church had no one to coach them, it had seemed a golden opportunity to involve Jason. And when a chance remark from Mitch at the picnic had informed her that Alex had been a pitcher on their high school team—well, that was too good to pass up.

She glanced at her watch. Alex should be home

from the plant soon, and this time they were playing where he could have no objection. The grassy lawn behind the garage was perfect for games, and even the most wildly hit ball couldn't damage anything. Or anyone. She thought of the Swiss businessman and winced.

But she wanted more than Alex's approval. She wanted his presence.

For Jason, she hurriedly reminded herself. This was for Jason, not for her. She stood back, watching the children, and tried not to think about what had happened between her and Alex on Saturday night. But it was useless. The memory wouldn't be denied.

Her cheeks heated at the thought of his kisses, and she could almost feel his strong arms around her, holding her protectively close. *Protected*—that was a good word for it. At a moment when reality had shattered around her, Alex had been a secure anchor.

That was all he had been, as far as he was concerned. She had to accept that. He'd been kind, and they'd both been a little carried away by the emotion of the moment. Maybe, for a few minutes, she'd dreamed their connection was something more.

But Alex's behavior in the days since had shown her the truth. He'd withdrawn from her, going back to his usual cool, urbane manner. The very tone of his voice had told her clearly that he regretted what had happened between them and had no intention of repeating that mistake.

At least he hadn't apologized. Her face burned at the thought. That would have been the final humiliation. He'd simply ignored the whole incident. Now she had to do the same.

She had to concentrate on the two people she'd come here to help. Aunt Maida would be home from the hospital soon, and Paula would have her hands full even with the aid of the church volunteers. And just as important, she had to make more headway with Jason.

She watched him toss the ball to Kristie, who promptly ducked. Jason had begun to smile again. Certainly that was progress. But she couldn't kid herself; the boy was worried about something. She could see it so clearly in the sadness that filled his eyes in unguarded moments. Whatever it was, he wasn't ready yet to confide in her. Maybe he never would be.

She wouldn't give up, she told herself as she went to help Kristie catch the ball. She'd come here to help Jason, and that's what she'd do, no matter who stood in the way.

"What's going on?" Alex's voice, coming so appropriately on the heels of her thought, startled her. Her heart cramped, and she took a firm grip on her emotions. *Be natural,* she ordered herself. *Pre-*

tend it never happened. She swung around, looking for signs of annoyance in his face. But he was smiling.

"Baseball practice."

"So I see." He came closer. He wore his usual white shirt, but his jacket was thrown over one arm and his striped tie was loosened. She reminded her heart not to feel anything.

"Aren't they too small for this?"

"Not according to my brothers. They put a baseball in my hand when I was three." She grinned. "I'm not advocating that, you understand. This is the peewee team from the church. They want to start playing, but they don't have a coach."

He raised an eyebrow. "How are they?"

She lowered her voice so the kids couldn't hear. "Well, they can't throw. They also can't catch or hit. But they have lots of enthusiasm."

"In that case, I wish you luck. Sounds as if their coach will need it."

"I didn't volunteer myself as coach." She braced herself for an explosion. "I volunteered you."

"Me!" For the moment he looked too dumbstruck to be angry.

"Mitch told me what a good player you were in high school. He thought this was a great idea."

"He would." Alex looked as if he was thinking up a suitable punishment for his friend. "I'm afraid it's out of the question." He turned away.

She wasn't going to let him off that easily, not where his son was concerned. "Why?"

He looked at her blankly. Apparently that was something people didn't often ask Alex Caine.

"Why?" she repeated. "Why is it out of the question? The kids need someone to work with them. You have the requisite skills."

"I've already made a donation to the program."

"The kids need someone to give time, not money. You have a son who wants to play. Why shouldn't that someone be you?"

"That should be obvious." He wore the expression she thought of as the *royal look*—the calm assumption that anything he chose to do wouldn't be questioned.

"Not to me, it isn't." Somewhat to her surprise, she realized that Saturday night's events had made her bolder where Alex was concerned. She wasn't sure why, but it seemed a step forward. "Explain it to me."

He sent a harassed look toward the children, who'd begun to gather around Paula. "You should know why. The business I'm working on right now is important. It requires all my concentration."

"All the more reason why you should be getting some physical activity and relaxation," she said promptly, ignoring a twinge of caution. She was pushing hard, and she'd probably have her head bitten off for her trouble.

He raised his eyebrows skeptically. "And you recommend coaching small children for relaxation?"

"Are you going to coach us, Dad?" Jason's eyes widened. "Will you?"

Kristie, carrot-colored ponytail bobbing, threw herself at his legs. "Please, please, please," she chanted, clearly not awed by his status.

Over the mob of small children, Alex shot her a look that was both laughing and annoyed. "I'll get you for this, Paula. You and Mitch both."

The tension inside her eased, and she smiled. "I'm not intimidated by threats. Let's see what your fastball looks like after all these years."

"Too fast for a bunch of seven-year-olds," he said. "Even at my advanced age. Suppose you start with batting practice, while I go change."

She nodded, starting onto the field as the children hurried to grab bats. But as she passed him, he caught her arm, drawing her close to him. His dark eyes sparkled with laughter, and her heart seemed to turn over. He didn't often look like that, and when he did, the effect was devastating.

"I meant it, Paula. You and Mitch are in trouble."

She willed her body not to betray the effect he had on her. "At least that means I've got the police chief on my side," she retorted.

Laughing, Alex headed toward the house, his suit

jacket slung over one shoulder. Paula kept her smile in place as she turned to the kids. Nobody was going to guess what she felt.

She'd created an opportunity for Alex and his son to grow closer, she reminded herself. That was what she'd intended. She hadn't intended to prove so clearly to herself that her feelings for Alex were completely out of control.

Paula had turned his world upside down, Alex thought as he raised the window shades in the old gardener's cottage the next afternoon. His studio flooded with light. Sunshine splashed across the wide, uneven oak flooring and touched the half-finished wood carving on the workbench.

He moved toward the carving of Jason he'd begun working on, his eyes assessing it, even while his mind continued on the by-now-familiar track. Paula, and the changes she'd brought to his life.

It was just like the last time she'd been in his house, he realized. She had a knack for turning the mansion into something other than the museum it so often felt like. She filled it with laughter, noise, small children. With Paula around, his son smiled.

The thought clutched his heart. Why hadn't he realized how little his son smiled? Jason's sober expression had become so habitual that Alex had begun to take it for granted—until Paula changed things.

He couldn't stop the smile that tugged at his own lips when he thought of that baseball team practice yesterday afternoon. She'd done it to involve him with Jason, of course, and she was remarkably good at not taking "no" for an answer.

But he'd had a surprise for her. If she wanted him to work with the children, she'd have to be involved, too. He wouldn't do it alone.

It was almost frightening, how much pleasure the idea of working with her gave him. He'd told himself there couldn't be anything between them for so many reasons, but she seemed to be breaking those walls down, one by one.

Unfortunately, the biggest wall still stood irrevocably between them. As long as she looked at him with hero-worship in her eyes, any other relationship was impossible.

He ran his hand over the grain of the carving, itching to get back to work on the piece. Carving soothed him, letting his mind wander while his fingers brought the wood to life.

A foolish waste of time. You have better things to do. It was remarkable how often the voice of his conscience sounded just like the voice of his father.

The knock at the door startled him. Quickly he tossed a cloth over the half-finished piece and went to answer.

"Paula." Somehow he wasn't surprised. He

hadn't satisfied her curiosity the last time she came to the cottage, and she wasn't one to give up.

She held Maida's wooden recipe box in her hands. "I found this on the kitchen counter. You've had it fixed." Her dimple flashed. "I'm so grateful. I hated the idea of explaining to her what happened."

"No problem."

He wanted to be happy for her, but the box was a reminder of her insistence that Jason had broken it deliberately. He'd thought of that each time he'd worked on it, and the accusation had leached the pleasure from the delicate repair job.

"If that's all…"

He should have closed the door more quickly. She moved past him as easily as if he hadn't spoken.

"Where did you have it fixed? I didn't realize there was a shop in town that did this sort of work."

He shrugged, groping for an answer. It was ridiculous to be so reticent about his hobby, but he couldn't seem to admit the truth to her.

In another second, the admission wasn't necessary. She saw the workbench. Her gaze shot from it to him.

"You repaired the box yourself, didn't you." She frowned. "I don't understand. Why didn't you tell me you were doing it?"

"I didn't think you'd be interested. What differ-

ence does it make who fixed it?'' He took a half
step toward the door, trying to ease her out. Having
her here brought her too far for comfort into his
inner life.

Paula ignored the hint, moving toward the draft-
ing table. Her eyes widened as she took in the papers scattered on it. ''Are these designs for the factory? I didn't realize you actually designed the
furniture you make.''

He swept the sheets together, unaccountably embarrassed. ''It's nothing. I don't do all the design-
ing, just a few of the lines.''

She touched the top sheet. ''That's the one Dieter
is interested in, isn't it?'' She looked up at him,
perplexed. ''Alex, I don't understand. Why are you
so reticent about it? If I had a gift like this, I'd be
proud.''

''The designs are part of my job. Nothing to be
excited about.'' He frowned down at the drawings.
''It's true they're an aspect of the attraction our
business has for Dieter, but certainly not all of it.
Don't get the idea that I'm the Michelangelo of the
furniture world.''

He couldn't suppress his embarrassment that
she'd found out. People at the plant knew, of
course, but they'd learned not to comment. He'd
started tinkering with designs when he was just a
kid. He'd quickly found that his father didn't consider that the proper role for a Caine. He was sup-

posed to run the plant, not play at being a draftsman.

"If you don't mind, Paula, I really have to get back to work. I'm a little short on time, especially since someone seems to have involved me in baseball practice."

He rather enjoyed the way she flushed and looked away.

"That's all I wanted. Just to say thank you."

She picked up the box, which she'd put on the table, and her elbow brushed the carving of Jason. Before he could grab it, the covering slid off.

Paula could only stare. She'd thought she understood Alex. She'd assumed she knew who he was—a rich man with no interest in anything other than his company and his family name.

But in the last few days she'd discovered facets of him she'd never expected. She'd seen the hero who had rescued her at the risk of his own life. She'd seen the gentle comforter who'd held her while she wept. And now she saw yet another side to the man she only thought she knew.

"It's beautiful." She reached out tentatively to touch the carving. Jason's face looked out of the warm, smooth wood. The piece was clearly not finished, but Alex had somehow suggested that lingering sadness that seemed a part of his son. She wondered if he even realized he'd portrayed that.

"It's not finished." Alex snatched up the cloth as if to hide this example of his artistry.

"No, I see that. But you've already caught his expression. That must be the most difficult thing." Her fingertips smoothed the figure's cheek. It was almost like touching the real thing, and her heart caught at the beauty of it. "Has Jason seen this yet?"

"No."

He flipped the cloth over the head, ignoring the fact that she still touched it. She took her hand away reluctantly.

"You want to wait until it's done, I suppose. But I'm sure he'd be fascinated at seeing his face appear in the wood."

Alex frowned, straightening a row of tools on the tabletop that didn't seem to need straightening. "I don't know that I'll show it to him. It's just something I've been playing around with."

"Not show him!" She reached out impulsively to touch his arm. "But it's wonderful. Any child would be thrilled." Didn't he realize that his love for his son came through in every line?

"It's more important that I provide properly for him, rather than wasting time on something like this." He looked as if the words tasted bitter in his mouth.

"Who said that?" she asked with sudden insight. "It sounds like a quote."

He shot her a look that was almost angry. "My father." He turned away from the workbench. "He had very little patience for wasting time. And he was right."

She wasn't sure how to respond to that. Probably she didn't have the right to say anything, but she couldn't seem to stop herself.

Lord, show me what to say to him. I didn't understand.

"It's not a waste of time to do something just for the love of it," she said.

His mouth tightened until he resembled the portrait of his father that hung in the library. "It is when there are more important things to be done. Like saving the company, for instance—"

For a brief instant she saw the pain reflected in his dark eyes.

"If this deal doesn't go through soon, I'll be letting down a great many people, in addition to my son."

She tried to find the words that would comfort him, but she didn't have any. She couldn't spout platitudes in the face of his pain. Had she been wrong to push his involvement with Jason?

No, I can't believe that, Lord. Important business deal or not, a son needs his father's attention far more than he needs status or money.

"You can't hold yourself responsible for the welfare of the whole town," she ventured.

His swift gesture of rejection told her that had been the wrong thing to say.

"I am responsible." His hands tightened on the edge of the table until the knuckles whitened and the tendons stood out like cords. "Bedford Creek has always depended on the Caine family for its livelihood. Nothing's changed. If the factory goes under, half the town will be unemployed. That is my responsibility."

"I'm sorry." It was all she could say. "I know you're doing your best for them. Everyone must know that."

But did they? Did anyone, outside of Mitch and Brett, perhaps, really look beneath the surface to see the real Alex Caine? Or did they look at that polished, cool exterior and envy the man who had everything?

The way she had, she had to confess. All these years she'd seen him as some sort of privileged being, immune to the struggles that beset ordinary people like her.

Now, for some reason she didn't understand, he'd given her a look at the man beneath the shining surface—the person whose life was a constant struggle to do what was expected of him.

The saddest thing was that he didn't see that being perfect was impossible. And he didn't see the barriers that it put between him and everyone else in his life, especially his son.

Chapter Eleven

Why wasn't her plan working? Paula had been so sure God had brought her here to help Jason. She'd been convinced it was her opportunity to atone for leaving so abruptly two years ago. But if this was what God intended, why was she failing? With a sudden flare of temper at her own inadequacy, she kicked one of the two-by-four boards she was using to build a temporary ramp to the housekeeper's cottage.

"Is that a new construction method?"

Her heart thudded into overdrive at the sound of Alex's voice, and she turned to annoyance in self-defense. "Must you sneak up on me that way?"

He crossed the grass from the pool. "You were too busy beating up that defenseless piece of wood to hear me. What's going on?"

"That's the question I wanted to ask you. What's going on? Why didn't you keep your promise to Jason?"

She could see in an instant that he'd forgotten it completely—a blank stare, followed quickly by comprehension, then embarrassment.

"You forgot." She knew she sounded accusing, and she didn't care. "You made a promise to your son, and you forgot." He had told Jason at breakfast he'd be home before supper to practice with the team. But four o'clock came and went, and no Alex.

Dismayed by the children's pensive little faces, Paula had tried to engage them in batting and fielding practice. The other children had responded, but Jason had thrown his glove down and walked off the field. She hadn't had the heart to reprimand him, knowing the depth of his disappointment.

"Where is he?" He looked around, as if he expected to find Jason still waiting. "Was he very upset?"

"Of course, he was upset! What would you expect? Don't you remember what it feels like when the most important person in your life lets you down?"

She knew she'd gone too far, and she regretted the words almost before they were out of her mouth. Given what Alex's father had been like, that had to be a sore spot. But it was too late to call her hasty words back.

Alex's mouth tightened. "I'll tell my son I'm sorry, Paula." His implication was clear—he didn't owe an apology to her. "Where is he?"

"Brett and Rebecca took him out for pizza with Kristie. They should be back in about an hour." She sounded like a sulky child, even to herself. She tried to be honest. Was her sharp retort on Jason's behalf? Or was she thinking of her own disappointment? Her newfound empathy for Alex had become frayed around the edges the last few days. His preoccupation with the business to the exclusion of everything and everyone in his life had become so intense that all her efforts to bring him and Jason together were evaporating. Jason withdrew; Alex withdrew—she seemed to be the only person in the house who was actually *there*.

She glanced at her watch. "Or sooner. I've been working on this thing longer than I thought."

"What exactly are you doing?" He picked up the two-by-four, sounding as relieved as she was to get away from the difficult subject on which they'd probably never agree. "Are you and Jason taking up carpentry?"

Now that she had the opportunity, she was reluctant to ask Alex for help. She folded the instructions. "The physical therapist said I should rig up a temporary ramp to the porch, for when Maida gets home. So she won't have to tackle the steps every time she wants to get out.''

He held out his hand. She fought down a flare of resentment at the imperious gesture and gave him the paper.

He scanned it quickly. "This doesn't look too difficult.''

"That's easy for you to say.'' Actually, it probably would be easy for him, given the unexpected skills she'd discovered he had. For that matter, she had yet to find the thing he didn't do well. "I'm afraid I must be mechanically challenged.''

"I'll take care of the ramp.'' Alex slipped the paper into his pocket before she could snatch it back.

"No, you won't.'' She planted her fists on her hips. "Aunt Maida asked me to handle this.''

He looked annoyed. She ought to be familiar with the expression by now, since he so often wore it when he looked at her.

Not when he kissed you, a small voice in her head reminded her. *Not when he held you.*

"I'm sure Maida expected you to take care of this by turning it over to me,'' Alex said. "She'd know I'd have the ramp installed properly.''

"You mean, I can't do it the way you want it done.'' The fact that she probably couldn't only added to her frustration.

"That's not what I meant. This isn't a good use

of your time, with the dinner party coming up. I'll have one of the carpenters from the plant stop by and do this.''

"Maida is my aunt. I'd rather provide for her myself.'' She was using anger as a shield, and she knew it. But anger was the safest emotion she could feel where Alex was concerned. At least when she was angry with him, she didn't have to remember what his arms felt like around her.

Alex studied her for a moment. His dark eyes were as intent as if he studied a business plan. "The cottage belongs to me,'' he said finally. "I will modify it for Maida's needs. Why is this so important to you?''

His question pierced the shield of her anger, and she struggled to get it back. "Because I'm used to doing things myself, not ordering someone else to do them. Some of us didn't grow up having all this—'' Her gesture took in the grounds, the pool, the mansion, maybe the whole town.

He didn't say anything, and she braced herself for an eruption. No, not an eruption. Alex was too cultivated to erupt. He'd give her the look that suggested she'd just crawled out from under a rock.

But he shook his head, suddenly looking tired. "That's not quite what you imagine it to be, Paula. I won't try to convince you of that, because I probably couldn't succeed.''

His calm, even tone brought a wave of embarrassment to her cheeks. Whether she was right or wrong, she shouldn't have spoken that way to him.

"I'm sorry. I—"

"You don't have to apologize for saying what you think of me. But I don't think you should be so proud of not accepting help, not when other people will have to pay the penalty for your pride."

"What are you talking about? What other people?"

"Maida, for one." He didn't sound angry, just matter-of-fact. "You'd rather build something you know won't work as well, so you can say you did it yourself."

His words stung, and she could tell he wasn't finished yet.

"And you won't let me help, even though I love Maida, too. I suppose that means my love is tainted by whatever privilege it is you imagine I possess. That's an odd kind of caring, Paula. I'm not sure Maida would approve."

She stared at him, her defenses crumbling and her eyes filling with tears. How could he cut her to the heart with a few words?

Alex's heart contracted when he saw the expression on Paula's face. He hadn't intended to hurt her, but he'd gone too far.

Maybe he was the one who needed to understand. He hadn't made any effort to find out why Paula felt as she did. He'd simply considered her stubborn independence an obstacle to what he knew was best. Did that mean he was as arrogant as she thought? He decided he didn't want to know the answer to that question.

"Paula." He reached out, wanting to touch her, knowing it was unwise. "I'm sorry. I don't want to hurt you. I want to understand."

She shook her head stubbornly, but her mouth trembled. "There's nothing to understand. I'm like everyone else."

Suddenly he didn't want to impose his will on hers or get his own way, even though he was convinced he was right. He just wanted to know what drove her.

"Tell me what's going on with you. Make me understand." He tried a smile. "In spite of the handicap of my imagined status, maybe I can."

He went to the steps, sat down and patted the spot next to him. That first night she'd done the same thing. Jason had sat next to her and connected with her in a way Alex still didn't quite understand.

The image of Jason's small face sent a twinge to his heart. Paula had been right about one thing: Alex had let Jason down tonight, and that was something he'd promised himself he wouldn't do. But Jason wasn't here now, and Paula was—a suddenly vulnerable Paula.

"Tell me what makes Paula Hansen tick," he said, trying to keep his voice light.

"Nothing out of the ordinary. Nothing important." She shrugged, obviously making an effort to sound casual, but she sat down next to him.

"It's important to you." For both their sakes, he had to stay detached. He had to be a friend, and nothing more. "Come on, Paula. Who are you really rebelling against?"

He knew at that moment that his shot in the dark had gone home. She crossed her arms over the Towson University T-shirt she wore, as if in self-defense. "I'm not. Not anymore, anyway."

"Why do I find that so hard to believe?" He tried to keep his voice gently teasing.

She shook her head. "Maybe I am a little overly independent. I don't think you'd understand why."

"Why wouldn't I?"

"Because you didn't grow up with four older brothers determined to protect you." There was a flicker of a smile at that.

"Doesn't sound so bad," he said, sure she hadn't yet reached the heart of the matter.

"Oh, really?" She did smile now. "Did you have an older brother who insisted on taking you to your first dance? Or one who threatened to beat up anyone who teased you? It got so bad, boys were afraid to smile at me."

"They loved you."

"They drove me crazy." She shook her head. "I had to fight them every step of the way. But it taught me to stand up for myself."

"And your father? Did you fight him, too?"

She rubbed her arms, the smile fading. "My father has some very old-fashioned ideas of what boys do and what girls do. Boys go places, they play sports, they get football scholarships if they want to go to college. Girls stay home. Girls are protected." Something in the timbre of her voice changed, betraying the emotion she seemed determined not to show. "I remember..."

He leaned a little closer, afraid to touch her because that might break the slender thread of connection between them. "What do you remember?" he said softly.

"I must have been about Jason's age." She looked down, her face soft and defenseless. "I had a teacher who really encouraged me. She recommended me for a special program for gifted kids. I remember coming home from school carrying the paper, so proud." Her hands clasped together.

He could almost see the little girl she'd been, blond braids to her shoulders, face alight with eagerness. "What happened?"

"My father refused to enroll me." Her face tightened. "The teacher even came to talk to him, but he wouldn't budge. I sat at the top of the stairs and listened. 'A waste of money,' he called it. He wasn't going to throw good money away on foolishness. It wasn't worth it.''

The vision of that little girl, huddled at the top of the stairs, hurt his heart. He knew what she'd felt when she'd heard those words. She'd felt *she* wasn't worth it.

Now, she'd reject sympathy. She'd interpret it as pity. ''He sounds like quite a reactionary. He and my father probably would have had a lot in common.''

She looked up, startled. Then, quite suddenly, she smiled. ''I don't know which of them would have been more shocked at that comparison.''

The tightness around his heart eased at her smile. ''I'd say you turned out remarkably well, considering the obstacles. You got your degree in spite of him, didn't you?''

''With Aunt Maida's help. You should have heard the battle between them over that. On second thought, if you'd been listening, you might have been able to hear it from Bedford Creek.''

''Maida is a special lady, isn't she. She's done as much, or more, for me over the years.''

Paula raised her eyebrows. ''Meaning you ought to be allowed to build the ramp for her?''

''I did have that in mind,'' he said. He sensed that she was eager to move away from the subject of her past.

Tears brightened her eyes for an instant, and she

blinked rapidly. "I guess even a rich man ought to be allowed to give a gift of love."

He ought to say something light in response, but he couldn't. He'd been wrong. He couldn't go this far into her life and stay detached. Like it or not, he'd begun to care for her too much. All he could think was how close they were, and how much he wanted to close that gap and kiss her.

She looked at him, and she had to be able to read the longing in his face. Her eyes darkened, and he seemed to hear her breath catch.

Car doors slammed, and children's voices echoed from the driveway.

Paula pulled away from him, her cheeks flushing. "They're back."

His first thought was that Brett had rotten timing. His second was that Brett actually had pretty good timing, because in another second Alex would have moved his relationship with Paula in a direction he'd promised not to go.

"Paula, how nice to run into you."

Paula, arms full of packages, stopped, surprised to be greeted by name on Main Street. Anne Donovan was just coming out of the candle shop. "I went to see Maida yesterday," Anne continued. "She's really doing well, isn't she?"

"The therapist says she'll be able to come home soon."

It felt like a deadline to Paula. The days were passing, and with them went whatever opportunity she had to do some good for Jason and his father. She'd thought that if she understood Alex better, she'd be able to help his son. Instead, she seemed only to have put her own heart in jeopardy. The memory of those moments on the steps the day before shimmered in her mind like a bubble about to burst.

"I'm so glad she's doing well," Anne said warmly. "Do you have time for a cup of coffee? We haven't had a chance to talk since you've been here." She nodded toward the café across the street.

Paula juggled packages to glance at her watch. "I do have half an hour before I pick up Jason. But I should get Alex's shirts—"

"Nonsense." Anne grabbed one of the bags. "You look as if you could use a break. Let Alex pick up his own shirts."

Paula couldn't help smiling as she followed the other woman across the street. Anne looked intimidating, with her glossy black hair and elegant clothes. But her easy friendliness was hard to resist.

Besides, she thought as Anne pushed open the door to the Bluebird Café, Anne's husband was one of Alex's closest friends. If anyone understood him, it was Mitch.

Anne dropped the packages on a blue-padded bench and slipped into the booth. Almost before

Paula sat down, an older woman slid coffee mugs in front of them and poured with a deft hand.

"What'll you have with the coffee? I've got some currant scones fresh from the oven." The woman poised a pencil over a pad.

"No, I—"

"Two currant scones," Anne said quickly. "Cassie, have you met Paula Hansen?"

The woman nodded briskly. "Work up at the big house, don't you? I'll be right out with those scones."

She whisked away toward the kitchen, and Anne gave Paula an apologetic smile.

"Sorry about that. But Cassie takes offense if you don't eat something. And given the way she talks, you don't want her annoyed with you."

"I guess there are some interesting pitfalls to living in a place as small as Bedford Creek."

Anne nodded. "I've been here nearly two years, and I still don't understand all the ins and outs of it. People imagine living in a small town is simple, but actually it's very complicated."

"Because everyone knows everyone else?"

"Even back a generation or two." Anne stirred sugar into her coffee. "Take Alex, for example. Everyone in town knows his family history."

"They've always been the people living in the big house on the hill," Paula agreed. *Where they can look down at everyone else.* She couldn't help the thought.

Cassie reappeared and put plates in front of them. Paula broke a corner off a feathery light scone. Still warm, as Cassie had promised.

"It can't be easy," Anne continued, slathering butter on her scone. "Having everyone in town interested in what you're doing. It might make you put a shield up for protection."

She looked at Anne with increased respect. "Yes, I guess it might."

"A few people probably get past that, if they try hard enough."

"Maybe." She could hear the doubt in her voice. She'd tried, hadn't she? But each time she got too close, Alex pulled away.

She seemed to see him leaning toward her on the porch steps. He'd have kissed her, if Brett and Rebecca hadn't arrived when they did. But that hadn't been regret she'd seen in his eyes when he pulled away. It had been relief. He'd been glad they were interrupted.

"Trust me." Anne smiled, dropping the pretense that this was a theoretical discussion. "Alex is worth the effort to get close to him. He and Mitch go back a long way. They—"

"Coffee and gossip?"

Paula looked up, barely able to restrain a gasp. She'd been so intent on what Anne was saying that she hadn't heard Alex come in. She probably looked guilty, but Anne just smiled and slid over on the seat.

"You can join us, if you want. We aren't bashing men, I promise."

Alex sat, then looked enquiringly across the table at Paula. "Where's Jason?"

"At the library story hour." She gestured toward her packages. "I was picking up a few things we need for the dinner party."

"She's allowed a coffee break, Alex." Anne's voice was silky. "You don't want to get a reputation as a slave driver, do you?"

"I'm finished," Paula said hurriedly, deciding she really didn't want to sit across from Alex with Anne looking on. The woman saw too much. "I'll take the scone with me to eat later." She wrapped a napkin around it.

"I'll walk out with you." Alex stood, putting a bill on the table before Paula could open her bag.

Once they were on the sidewalk outside, she expected Alex to head down toward the plant. Instead, he walked beside her as she made her way uphill to the tiny library. In Bedford Creek, it seemed you were always going either uphill or down.

When he didn't say anything for half a block, she began to feel nervous. "Is something wrong?"

He looked at her blankly. "Why should anything be wrong?"

"Well, I thought you were on your way back to the office."

His rare, charming smile was like the sun coming out on a cloudy day. "I should be. But I'm playing hooky, just for the moment."

She smiled back, the tension inside her relaxing. Alex was treating her like a friend, instead of a housekeeper. That was the most she could expect, and she shouldn't let herself have silly dreams of something more. But there was something unresolved between them, and maybe this was a good time to bring it up.

"There's something I've been wanting to say to you all week, and I've never had the chance."

"What?" His dark eyes grew wary, as if expecting the worst.

"You don't need to look like that." She smiled. "It's not anything bad. It's just…I wanted to tell you how much I appreciate what you did in the accident. 'Thank you' doesn't seem enough to say to someone who saved your life."

"That's not necessary." His tone was curt, and he turned away almost before the words were out. "I have to get back to the plant." He strode off, leaving her staring after him.

One instant he'd been smiling down at her, warm and approachable. The next he'd turned into a cold, distant stranger.

Chapter Twelve

By the next day, Paula had had twenty-four hours to think about that exchange with Alex on the street, and she still didn't understand his reaction. She stood at the linen closet, counting out napkins for the dinner, trying to concentrate on anything but the memory of the look on Alex's face when he'd turned away from her.

She clenched the napkins, as if she could use them to wipe away the image. It didn't work. Nothing would push it out of her mind, not even the rush and tension of the dinner preparations.

The linens stacked carefully in her arms, she started down the stairs. She hadn't taken two steps into the downstairs hallway before the caterer grabbed her arm, nearly sending the clean linens to the floor.

"Ms. Hansen... Oh, sorry." The woman caught the stack as it toppled. "I have to talk with you."

"Is something wrong?" Judging by the expression on Janine Laker's face, something was amiss, and Paula braced herself. Janine and her brother were supposed to be the best caterers in town, in addition to running the finest restaurant. They'd do a wonderful job, everyone said, but they had high expectations of the resident staff. Meaning her.

"The cleaning people are supposed to be finished in here." Janine glared at the man running a vacuum in the dining room. "And the flowers haven't arrived yet. We can't finish the tables without the flowers."

"I'll take care of it." Paula tried to sound soothing. "The cleaners will be finished momentarily, and I'll see to the flowers."

An answering glare from the cleaner suggested he wouldn't welcome any advice on finishing his job, and Janine didn't look as reassured as she hoped.

"We want everything to be perfect when we do a dinner," Janine said. "Everything."

"I'm sure it will be." Paula hoped she sounded calmer than she felt. "You can leave the dining room to me."

Looking only partially appeased, Janine disappeared into the kitchen.

Cleaners, florist, table settings. She shook her

head, remembering the moment in which she'd assured herself that this would be easy. Give her thirty rambunctious five-year-olds, and she knew what to do. Making the arrangements for a formal dinner party was something else again.

Finally the cleaners were finished and out the door, taking their equipment with them. The florist had delivered the centerpiece, and delightful aromas had begun to float from the kitchen. Paula stood back, looking with admiration at the long table. Pristine white linen covered it, with not an errant crease in sight. Bone china reflected light back toward the chandelier, and cut-glass tumblers glistened.

Her gaze lingered on the massive chair at the head of the table. Alex would sit there, elegant and in control. Candlelight would flicker, while soft music played in the background. With a guilty start, she realized she was picturing herself seated at that table, too. Firmly putting that image from her mind, she began folding napkins.

Just as she finished, Alex came in. His swift gaze assessed the room.

"Is everything ready?" He frowned, looking at the table as if he expected a flaw.

"Everything is coming along fine," she said. "You don't need to worry." At least, she certainly hoped that was true. She ran her mind over her lists again, nervously checking to see that everything had been done.

"I don't see any place cards." Alex strode to the table, his frown deepening. "I told you we'd need place cards." His tone suggested that only the most inept of housekeepers would neglect something so important. And maybe that he hadn't expected any better from her.

Paula snatched up the calligraphy place cards she'd left on the window sill and handed them to him. "Place cards," she said.

He had the grace to look embarrassed. "I thought you'd forgotten them."

"You didn't tell me how you wanted the seating arranged, so I was waiting until you arrived to put them out."

She tried to feel resentment, because that was safer than looking at her true emotions. Unfortunately she knew what they were—longing, hurt, love.

Alex looked down at the place cards in his hand, because that way he didn't have to look at Paula's face. She'd hand-lettered each card in graceful script, and his guilt deepened. She'd done more than he'd asked, and all he'd done in return was bark at her.

"I'm sorry." *Sorry I snapped at you because I*

wanted to keep some space between us. "Let's decide how best to arrange the table."

"Fine."

Her back was stiff as she walked to the long table, her tone making it clear that he wasn't forgiven yet.

"I assume you want Mr. Dieter on your right."

He nodded, handing her the card. He'd thought he knew what his attitude toward Paula had to be. But unfortunately, just seeing her had thrown his careful, well-ordered plans into disarray. He'd been so aghast at the surge of feelings she produced that he'd barked at her in self-defense.

Yesterday he'd let himself get too close, again. He'd almost let himself think a relationship between them might work. Then she'd brought up the crash and looked at him as if he were a hero. That attitude wasn't a recipe for happiness—it was a recipe for disaster.

"It's just not going to be perfect," Paula said. He gave her a startled look, then realized she was talking about the table.

"The arrangement?"

She shrugged. "Too many men and not enough women. Even I know the table should be balanced, but you just can't do it."

He didn't know what to say to the implicit self-criticism in her words. He hadn't intended to make her feel inadequate. She was doing a good job, and he hadn't realized before how difficult it was. Maida had always made things look easy.

"Do you think this will work?" She put the last card in place.

He saw the concern in her eyes, and it touched his heart. "It will be fine." He had a sudden picture of Paula in a soft evening dress instead of her usual jeans and T-shirt, sitting across from him at the table, the candlelight reflected in her deep green eyes. "If you—"

A commotion erupted in the hallway, composed of thudding feet and puppy yelps.

"Nugget, come back here!"

It sounded as if Jason had jumped down the last three or four steps, Alex thought. Jason had never come down the steps that way before Paula entered their lives. Why hadn't it ever occurred to him that a small boy wasn't supposed to be decorous?

Paula reached the hall a few steps before him and bent to corral the golden fur ball that was Nugget. She knelt, holding the puppy, until Jason reached her and grabbed Nugget's collar.

"Hey, Jason, I thought we decided Nugget would stay outside today." Her voice was soft, her face on a level with his son's.

Jason's lower lip came out in a pout. "Why can't he be in here? I want him to."

Paula stroked the puppy. "Well, mostly because there are a lot of strangers in and out today. That's upsetting for a puppy. And we put candy out in dishes for the guests. What if Nugget got some of it? Did you know it could make him sick?''

"I wouldn't do anything to let him get sick." Jason's pout disappeared. "Come on, Nugget. Let's go out back and play. I'll throw the ball for you."

Boy and dog pounded toward the door, not even noticing Alex, who tried to swallow the lump in his throat. Paula was so good with his son, so easy and unaffected. Jason responded to her better than he had to anyone in a long time.

"You must be a very good teacher," he said.

She looked up, as surprised as if she'd forgotten he was there, and got up quickly. "I am, as a matter of fact." She smiled, and the tension between them vanished. "But what brought that on?"

"You're good with Jason." He wanted to say more—to say she'd brought laughter back to his son—but he couldn't form the words.

Paula shrugged. "I like him. I think he likes me." Her gaze slid away from his, and he knew she was hiding something.

"And?" he prompted.

"I guess…" She hesitated. "I guess I feel I let him down, going away so suddenly the last time I was here. I'd like to make up for that, if I can."

Regret was a cold hand around his heart. He'd been the reason she'd left so abruptly then, he was sure of it. He didn't want to make the same mistake again. But he wanted to show her how much he appreciated her efforts for Jason. For him.

"About the dinner tonight—" He stopped. Was he doing the right thing? A wave of rebellion swept over him. This might not be the proper thing, but he felt quite sure it was right. "Will you do me the honor of joining the guests?"

Either she'd heard him wrong, or she'd misunderstood him. It almost sounded as if Alex were inviting her to be a guest at his dinner. "What did you say?"

"I want you to join us." Alex gestured toward the table. "You can easily fit another place setting there, since Dieter didn't bring as many people as I thought he might." He paused. "Can't you?"

"Well, yes." Pleasure swept through her. Alex wanted her to join in something that was important to him. *Don't read too much into this,* some part of her mind cautioned. "But why do you want me to attend?"

For a moment he looked disconcerted, as if he hadn't expected her to ask the question. "You said yourself the table was unbalanced. Not enough women."

"You could have asked another woman from the office."

"Yes, I could have, but I didn't." He gave her

that rare smile. "I want you to come, Paula. Please."

A wave of warmth flooded her. "In that case, I'd like to." She turned back to the table, to hide any trace of embarrassment. "I can add another setting here."

She felt his gaze on her as she rearranged the place settings, and her hands became clumsy in response. What did he see when he looked at her?

"Paula, there's just one thing." He was frowning again, looking at her jeans. "You do have something else to wear, don't you?"

Well, that seemed to be the answer to how he saw her—as someone who didn't know how to dress. Before she could respond, someone did it for her.

"Alex, that's not a question to ask a woman." Anne Donovan came in through the kitchen door, amusement filling her deep blue eyes. She gestured toward the kitchen. "The caterers let me in. I hope you don't mind."

Alex smiled, kissing her cheek lightly. "You're always welcome. Is that for me?" He nodded toward the sheaf of papers in her hand.

"No, it's for Paula. A list with phone numbers of people who are going to bring food in or help out when Maida comes home. I thought she might be feeling overwhelmed at the moment." She shot a teasing glance at Alex. "And your insults don't help."

He raised his hands as if to shield himself from attack. "I just thought Paula might not have come prepared for a dinner party."

Paula did a quick mental inventory of the clothes she'd brought with her. Was there anything suitable for dinner with Alex's business associates? Did she even *own* anything suitable?

"That's not a problem," Anne said. "If she doesn't have anything with her, we're about the same size. But Alex, if Paula is going to attend this business dinner, she has to have time to get ready. You can't expect her to make all the arrangements, take care of Jason, and then scramble into her clothes."

Paula tensed for one of Alex's polite putdowns, but it didn't come. Anne, like her husband, seemed to be one of the few people who could treat Alex like a human being. He shook his head, smiling.

"You're right as always. Paula, please take all the time you need. I'm sure the caterers know what they're doing, and I'll see to Jason."

"And the puppy," Anne prompted.

"And the puppy," Alex agreed. He shook his head. "I don't know how Mitch managed to survive before you came to town."

"Not as well as he does now," Anne said, her mouth softening at the mention of her husband. She linked her arm through Paula's. "Come on. Let's decide what you're wearing tonight."

Bemused at Anne's management, Paula let herself be led through the kitchen and out onto the patio. There she stopped, common sense reasserting itself.

"Alex was right. I really don't have anything with me to wear." She looked down at her jeans. "And even if I did, it wouldn't be suitable for Alex's high-powered business types."

"Relax." Anne patted her arm. "We really are about the same size, and I have a closet full of clothes from when I used to work with some of those high-powered business types." She smiled. "Believe me, those clothes don't get much of an outing in Bedford Creek. I'll find an outfit for you to wear."

"But I couldn't. What if I spilled something on it?"

"Everything can be cleaned." Anne didn't seem concerned. "I'll run home and bring a couple of choices back. Meanwhile, you go run yourself a bubble bath." Her face lit with laughter. "We're going to knock Alex for a loop, believe me."

Paula still found the turn of events hard to believe two hours later, when she stood in front of the full-length mirror in Maida's cottage.

"That's it." Anne, sitting behind her on the twin

bed, beamed with satisfaction. "That outfit was never quite right for me, but on you it's absolutely perfect."

Paula ran her hand down the length of shimmering aqua silk. "Are you sure you want to lend this? It's so lovely." It was the kind of dress she'd look at in the windows of the most exclusive shops—look at and walk on, knowing she couldn't afford it.

"I'm positive." Anne got up, a small box in her hand. "I brought the jewelry I wore with it, since you probably don't have much with you for the summer."

"What a tactful way of putting it." Paula smiled.

Anne held the dangling crystal drops at Paula's ears. "What do you think? They're the perfect touch, aren't they?"

Paula looked again at the image in the mirror. If she blinked, that elegant stranger might disappear. She laughed suddenly. "Aunt Maida would say, 'Fine feathers don't make fine birds.'"

"In this case, the fine feathers are just bringing out the beauty that's already there." Anne gave her a quick hug. "You really will dazzle them."

Paula glanced at the clock, and a wave of pure panic swept over her. "It's almost time. What on earth am I going to say to those people? I don't know anything about business."

"They're just people," Anne said. "Encourage

them to talk about themselves, and they'll be happy." She turned toward the door. "You can't back out now. Alex is counting on you."

"Right." Paula took a deep breath. She could do this. Anne was right—they were just people.

They walked back to the mansion together, but Anne stopped at the back door. "I'd better get home. Wish I could be a fly on the wall, though. I'd give anything to watch Alex's face when he sees you."

Hand on the door, Paula paused, thinking about Anne's words. That was why she stood here, half eager, half afraid. Because she wanted Alex to see her in a new way. Not as a housekeeper, not as a nanny, not as his assistant baseball coach. She wanted him to see her as a woman—a woman he could love.

Chapter Thirteen

Where was Paula? Alex wondered for perhaps the twentieth time, as he stood in the front hallway, greeting his guests. She'd done a wonderful job of organizing this affair. The old house shone with an unusually welcoming air. He tried to analyze the change. Perhaps it was the bowl of fresh-cut flowers on the hall table—from the garden, he realized, not the florist. Or maybe it was the way Janine circulated, at Paula's suggestion, offering shrimp and cheese puffs from a tray as guests arrived.

Paula had put her own stamp on this affair. The only thing missing was Paula herself.

He silently counted heads. Everyone else had arrived, including Christian Dieter and his staff. Dieter, a rotund elderly man whose cherubic expression was belied by a pair of shrewd ice-blue eyes, seemed genuinely pleased at being entertained in Alex's home.

Alex pressed down a wave of apprehension. No one must know from his demeanor how important this night was to him. He should be concentrating on Dieter, not worrying because Paula hadn't shown up yet.

Maybe she'd lost her nerve at the thought of participating. It hadn't occurred to him at the time that he might be putting additional pressure on her with his invitation. He'd just wanted to show her how much he appreciated her, not put her on the spot. She might have balked at the thought of coming to an elegant dinner party in a hand-me-down dress.

Just then, the door to the rear of the house swung open, and Paula walked into the hallway. She stopped directly under the crystal chandelier his great-grandfather had brought back from Germany.

The breath went out of him. She was beautiful. The blond curls that usually tumbled around her face had been swept back into a sophisticated style, and crystal drops dangled from her ears and around her neck, rivaling the chandelier for brilliance. The dress, an elegant length of aqua silk, molded her slender form, making her skin glow with a golden sheen, as if she'd brought the sunlight in with her.

He wasn't the only one she'd struck dumb, he realized. Dieter stood silent, interrupted in the midst of a story he'd been telling. With a brief nod, he dismissed the aide at his elbow and moved toward Paula.

It was high time Alex stopped staring, too. Anyone who'd been watching him would have known that Paula Hansen had just made him feel like an awkward kid instead of the company president.

He arrived at Paula's side in time to hear Dieter introducing himself.

"I am Christian Dieter." The man captured Paula's hand and held it in both of his. "I regret that I have not yet been introduced to you."

Paula's smile looked a bit strained. "I'm Paula Hansen, Mr. Dieter. It's a pleasure to meet you."

Dieter raised his eyebrows as he looked at Alex. "Where have you been hiding this lovely lady since our arrival?"

"I'm Alex's—"

"I'm afraid Paula has been very busy lately." Alex put his hand lightly on her waist, identifying his feeling with some surprise—possessiveness. He shouldn't feel that way about her, but he couldn't deny it. "Paula is a friend who's been helping me this summer."

"Lucky man," Dieter murmured, "to have such a lovely helper. And what do you do, Ms. Hansen, when you are not helping your friends?"

"I'm a teacher."

Paula drew slightly away from Alex, as if to put some space between them, but he increased the pressure of his hand, unwilling to let her go. He thought the faintest flush touched her cheeks.

"I teach kindergarten at a school in Baltimore."

"Inner Harbor," Dieter exclaimed, beaming. "I visited your city once on business. It's lovely."

Alex wondered, a little sourly, if there was anything Dieter didn't find lovely. Janine arrived at his elbow with a tray, distracting Dieter. As the man began asking Janine to identify the various tidbits, Alex drew Paula away from them a step or two.

She looked up at him, her eyebrows lifting. "A friend?" she asked softly.

He thought there was a slightly edgy undertone to her voice. "Aren't you a friend?" he countered, enjoying the way her green eyes sparkled.

Her chin tilted at a stubborn angle. "Maybe. But I'm also your housekeeper, remember? Are you embarrassed to tell Mr. Dieter that?"

She tried again to pull away from him, but he captured her hand. "Not at all. But tonight you're not my housekeeper. You're my guest."

Her hand twisted in his, and he tightened his fingers. They were engaged in a battle, locked in a private circle, just the two of them. The buzz of conversation in the hallway only served to isolate them together.

Paula looked up at him, emotions warring in her face. "I don't want people to get the wrong idea. They might think—"

She stopped, as if afraid to put it into words.

"They might think we're together," he finished for her. "Would that be so terrible?"

"I don't know." She met his gaze with a challenge in those clear green eyes. "Would it?"

Alarm bells seemed to be going off in his mind, and he ruthlessly suppressed them.

"Not at all," he said softly. He raised her hand, holding it in both of his. "Besides, if I don't lay claim to you, every man here will be trying to impress you. Then how will we get any work done at all?"

"That would be a problem." Her gaze never left his, and the things they weren't saying hovered in the air between them.

"We can't have that," he said. He brought her hand to his lips and kissed it, feeling her smooth skin warm to his touch. The others receded into the distance, as vague and insubstantial as flickering images on an old newsreel.

He heard her breath go out in a little sigh.

"No." She barely breathed the word. "I guess we can't."

Paula was adrift in an ocean in which only she and Alex were real. She knew the others were there, of course. She heard the murmur of polite conversation and the quiet background music she'd started. But all she really felt, all she really knew, was the touch of Alex's lips against her skin.

"Ms. Hansen." Janine's voice was low but insistent.

Paula forced her gaze away from Alex, made herself turn and smile. Janine, neat in a black skirt and white silk blouse, didn't look convinced. Her dark eyes held a certain speculative expression. Paula stiffened. What was the woman thinking?

For that matter, what was everyone else thinking? The whole room could have noticed the byplay between her and Alex. She took a cautious look around, but the others seemed engrossed in their own conversations.

"Dinner is ready to serve, Ms. Hansen."

Paula tried to look as if she received messages like that every day. She suspected Janine wasn't fooled.

"We'll be right in." She turned to Alex, trying to keep from blushing as her gaze met his. "Will you get people moving to the dining room?"

"I will." He touched her arm. "And you'll go in with me."

The wonder was that she actually arrived at the table without tripping over her heels. And she couldn't blame it on the fact that she'd been wearing sneakers all summer. Alex's grasp was sending messages tingling along her skin, distracting her so that the simplest action seemed difficult. Luckily she'd seated herself along the side of the long table, where she wouldn't have to meet his gaze throughout the meal.

But Alex led her to the chair opposite his, quietly indicating places to his guests as he did so. He pulled out the chair, and she shook her head.

"This isn't mine," she murmured.

He nodded to the place card. "It is now," he said.

He must have changed them around, and she could hardly try to rearrange the seating at this point. She slid into the seat he held out, very aware of his strong hands brushing her shoulders. He bent over as he seated her, his face so close to hers that she felt the warmth radiating from his skin.

"You're my hostess," he said softly, his breath caressing her cheek. "Naturally you'll sit opposite me." Then he straightened, and her skin felt cold where his breath had been.

She sat very straight as he went to the head of the table, trying not to watch him. How she was going to get through this evening without everyone there knowing she loved him, she couldn't imagine.

Love. The word echoed in her mind, shaking her. No, she couldn't let herself think things like that. Resolutely she turned to the man seated on her right.

Dieter's second-in-command looked far too young for his position, and much too stiff to carry on a conversation with her. After several futile attempts to find something they had in common, Paula remembered Anne's advice.

"Do you have a family back in Zurich?" she asked, not sure whether it was common for European men to wear wedding bands.

He beamed. "My wife and I have a baby daughter. She is just six months old."

It took very little prompting to get him going then. As he told her story after story designed to show that young Elissa was surely the brightest baby who'd ever been born, Paula decided that Anne had been right. He was really just a person.

He produced photos of a round-faced, solemn infant, and talked about how much he missed his family when he had to travel with Uncle Christian on business. She nodded, made encouraging noises and tried not to watch Alex.

But it was useless. She couldn't prevent her gaze from being drawn to him, any more than a compass could prevent its needle from pointing north.

She forced herself to look away, glancing around the table. Janine and her brother had outdone themselves, and the salmon *en croute* had been an inspired choice for the entrée. Dieter ate and gestured, his face growing more relaxed by the moment. He leaned toward Alex, nodding, and she could tell by the smallest of things—the set of Alex's mouth, the movement of his hand—that he was pleased.

Where had it come from, that unconscious ability to read his mood? When had every line, every gesture, become familiar and dear to her?

Love, she thought again, and this time the word didn't seem quite so frightening. Alex looked up just then and caught her watching him. He gave her a small, private smile.

Something strong and tangible seemed to run the length of the table between them. The connection was so palpable that she felt everyone at the table must have been able to see it. It was so strong it gripped her heart as if it would never let go.

"It has been a great pleasure. Thank you again." Dieter beamed at Paula, clasping her hand, as he and his entourage finally headed out the door.

She'd felt stiff, standing next to Alex in the gracious center hallway, telling his guests good-night as if she and Alex were a couple. But Alex had made it clear that was what he expected, and no one else seemed surprised. Of course, Dieter and his people didn't know what her true position was here, and those who worked for Alex apparently accepted what he did without question. It was his house, his company, his town.

When Alex finally closed the door, she should have felt relief, but she didn't. All she could think was that they were alone together, and there were too many conflicting feelings bouncing around inside her for comfort.

"I should check the kitchen," she began, but Alex caught her hand before she could move in that direction.

"Janine and her crew will leave everything spotless. They always do, and she wouldn't like the suggestion that you had to check on her."

"No, I didn't mean that." *I meant the excuse would get me out of your presence until I figure out what's happening between us.*

Alex loosened his tie. "It went well tonight. Thank you, Paula. For everything."

She nodded. Did "everything" include the way he'd teased her? The moment when he'd kissed her hand? Her skin tingled at the memory. Maybe she'd better find a safer topic of conversation.

"What about Dieter? I saw the two of you talking at dinner, and he looked receptive."

"Very receptive." His face relaxed in a smile. "I'm beginning to think we might pull this off. And if we do, I owe you thanks for that, too. I don't know how I'd have gotten through these past weeks if you hadn't been here."

"I was glad to fill in for Aunt Maida in any way I could." That sounded hopelessly stilted, and it wasn't what she wanted to say at all. What she wanted to say was that she'd do anything for him.

But how could she, when she didn't know how he felt?

She glanced at her watch. "Well, maybe I'd better go." She gestured to the silk dress. "I think it's time for Cinderella to turn back into a pumpkin."

"That isn't how the story goes, is it?" He still held her hand loosely, and she didn't want to pull away.

"Close enough," she said.

"I'll walk you out."

His hand was warm against her waist as they pushed through the swinging door into the back of the house. From the kitchen came the clatter of pans and the sound of voices. Alex guided her out the back door to the patio.

The nearly full moon sent a silver path along the surface of the pool, and the stars clustered thickly, far brighter than they ever were when seen from the city. She walked beside Alex, hearing the faint unevenness in his steps that was the only hint of his leg injury.

They stopped at the end of the pool. The kitchen window cast a golden oblong onto the flagstones, but other than that everything was dark and quiet. The silver birch bent gracefully opposite them, its white bark sketching a ghostly figure against the gazebo.

"It's a beautiful night," she murmured. Maybe

speech would interrupt the flood of feelings that surged through her. She shivered a little.

"You're cold," Alex said instantly. Before she could object, he'd shed his suit coat. "Put this on. Lovely as it is, I don't think that silk is going to keep you warm."

He draped the coat over her shoulders. It fell around her, still warm with the heat of his body. The fine wool carried a faint, musky scent that seemed to say his name.

She looked up. Alex was a dark silhouette against the darker night. She couldn't make out his expression, but whatever she imagined of his face took her breath away. She wanted to put her palms on his white shirt front, feel his heart beating....

"I should go in." Her voice sounded soft and uncertain, not at all like her.

"Maybe you should," he murmured, but his grip tightened on her hands.

"Jason will be up early. I really..." She lost whatever she'd been about to say when Alex drew her slowly against him.

His shirt was smooth against her hands, and through it she could feel the warmth of his body. For a heartbeat he just held her close. Then he stroked her face, his fingertips gentle against her skin, and emotion ricocheted through her. She cared so much for him. She'd tried to deny it, but it was no use.

He tipped her chin back, his touch insistent, and then his lips found hers. Gentle, so gentle. The kiss was tentative, questioning, as if he gave her every opportunity to draw away if that was what she wanted.

But she couldn't. Her arms slid around him almost without conscious volition, and every cell in her seemed to sing. She drew him closer. Paula's heart pounded, so full it seemed it could hold no more. She loved him, and she wanted to stay in his arms forever.

He pulled away, tearing his lips from hers. "No."

She could only stare at him, trying to read his expression through the gloom, trying to understand through the tumult in her heart. It was what had happened before. He'd kissed her in the moonlight, and then he had pulled away, apologized, tried to pretend it had never happened.

But he couldn't get away with denying it this time. Two years ago she'd let him, but not now. Not when she saw how he wanted to hold her. That gave her courage.

"Why?" She caught his arms when he would have pulled away, held him close. He couldn't break free without hurting her, and she knew he wouldn't do that. "Just tell me why. You can't say you don't want this, because I don't believe it."

His breath sounded ragged. "Maybe I do. But I'm not the hero you think I am, Paula. I'm not."

Her first impulse was to argue, to point out that he'd saved her life at the risk of his own. But some instinct told her that was the wrong thing to say. For whatever reason, he couldn't see himself in that light. And it was important to him. She could feel how important in the tension under her hands.

"That's good," she said quietly. "Because I don't want a hero. Just you, Alex. Just you."

Chapter Fourteen

Paula came awake slowly, trying without success to hold on to the fragments of a dream. She couldn't remember what the image had been, but she knew it was happy. She still felt warm and protected in its aftermath. Automatically she reached out for Nugget, but her hand didn't encounter a furry object in the puppy's usual sleeping spot.

She opened her eyes. Nugget wasn't there. Then she remembered. Alex had said the puppy could spend the night with Jason, so she could concentrate on the dinner party.

She sat up, memories flooding her—last night, the dinner, those moments on the patio when Alex had kissed her and she'd felt as if she'd come home.

Be careful, a faint, cautious voice urged in the back of her mind. *Be careful with your heart. It's a long way from kisses in the moonlight to happily ever after.*

That was probably good advice. Unfortunately, she suspected it was far too late for her to heed it.

She glanced at the clock, then swung off the bed and reached for her clothes. She was late. Alex and Jason would be expecting their breakfast.

A few minutes later, she hurried into the kitchen, half expecting to find Alex already in search of his morning coffee. But the kitchen was spotless and empty. One of Maida's refrigerator magnets held a note in Alex's bold hand.

She snatched the paper, unable to prevent a silly little catch to her breath. But the brisk message, saying he'd had a meeting and had left early, didn't give any indication its writer had been thinking of late-night kisses.

Paula pressed down a surge of disappointment. She'd better get Jason up and have him take Nugget outside while she fixed his breakfast.

The front area of the mansion, back to its usual silence, seemed to reject the memory of yesterday's hustle and the evening's elegance. She went quickly up the stairs to Jason's room and called out his name, tapping as she opened the door.

But Jason wasn't there. And when she went to the window that overlooked the pool and the back lawn, she still saw no sign of boy or dog.

Paula had just started down the stairs when she

paused, listening. Something disturbed the stillness. Then she heard it—the smallest yelp, instantly shushed. The sound came from the circular staircase that led to the cupola on top of the house.

She went quickly to the steps and looked up, squinting against the sunshine pouring toward her through the windows of the octagonal cupola. "Jason?"

Nugget barked in answer. What was going on? Surely the puppy hadn't gone up there alone. She hurried up the steep, tight spiral.

She reached the top step and stood on the cupola floor, then instantly regretted it. The tall windows on every side of the octagonal chamber gave views of the town, the river far below, and the mountain ridges soaring above. Standing there was like flying above the valley.

Jason sat scrunched into a ball, his face turned away from her. She sat, scooting close enough to Jason to touch him.

Please, Father, please. Show me what this child needs from me.

"Hey." She touched his shoulder gently. "What's going on? You can tell me."

He moved slightly, then buried his face again, but not before she'd seen the tears in his eyes.

"Jason, what is it? Are you hurt?"

He shook his head, holding out against her for another moment. Then, quite suddenly, he looked up. "I saw you." He hurled the words at her accusingly.

"You saw me?" What on earth had him so upset?

"I saw you," he said again. "Last night. From my window. You were kissing my daddy."

Her heart turned over. Jason's bedroom windows overlooked the patio. He'd obviously been looking out. What he'd been doing up that late wasn't the point. He'd seen them, and he was upset.

She tried to respond calmly, not making too much of it. "Your dad walked out with me after the party. Yes, we did kiss. Grown-ups do that sometimes when they like each other. It doesn't mean..."

She couldn't make herself say that kissing Alex didn't mean anything, because that wouldn't be true. His kisses had meant a great deal to her. Whether they meant the same to Alex was still to be determined.

"It's just like before." Jason's face was blotchy with tears. "That's what you did before, and then you went away."

His words pierced her heart. Jason was right—although he couldn't possibly know or understand the reasons. She'd kissed Alex, and she'd left when he made it clear that kiss had been a mistake. What else could she have done? After all, she had a little pride—

She stopped, the word resonating to her very soul. *Pride.* Was that what it had been? Was that what had put her on that airplane, intending to scurry back to Baltimore? She didn't want to believe that about herself.

Jason's the important person now. Do your soul-searching later.

"Jason, I'm sorry I went away." She spoke slowly, choosing her words carefully. Each one should be as true as she could make it. "I made a mistake, and I let you down. I'm sorry."

He shook his head violently. "Everybody goes away. It's my fault."

She stared at him, appalled that this precious child could think it his fault people had let him down. *His mother. Then me. I let him learn to rely on me, and then I left. I ran away because I couldn't face the emotional pain of staying.*

"Jason, it's not your fault. Please, believe me. Talk to me about this." She tried to touch him again, but he shook off her hand and scrambled to his feet.

"I won't talk to you!" He shouted it, the hurt in his eyes turning suddenly to anger. "I won't! You'll just go away again!"

He turned and thundered down the steps.

She sat where she was, trying to grasp what was happening. Nugget stood at the top of the steps, whining, then came to her and nudged her hand.

She gathered him into her arms, understanding why Jason had been up here hugging him. Comfort. The child had been looking for the comfort he wasn't getting from the adults in his life.

Is that what I've been doing, Lord? Asking the question was painful. *Have I been running away? Has my pride in being independent just been a cover for being afraid?*

She felt as if God had taken her heart, with all its pitiful little secrets, and held it up to His sunlight, pouring through the high windows. She wasn't very happy with what she saw.

She'd hurt Jason through her cowardice. She'd run away when she should have faced things. Faced Alex. If he hadn't cared for her then, if he didn't care for her now, she had to face it and go on. And right now Jason's needs had to come first.

Certainty pooled in her. She knew what God expected of her. The child was hurting, and he was trying to hide that pain, probably because he saw his father do the same thing.

It's my fault. Jason's words put a lump in her throat. He wouldn't tell her what he meant or why he believed that. His father was the only one who could possibly get to the bottom of this.

She had to make Alex see the truth about his son. Her heart seemed to cramp. It didn't take much imagination to know how Alex would react. Confronting him could put an end to any hope she might cherish that he returned her love.

She didn't have a choice. She had to do this, and soon, no matter what the cost.

Alex walked into the house, realizing he half expected to hear the noisy thud of Jason's feet on the oak stairwell or find Paula chasing an errant puppy across the Italian marble floor. But the Caine mansion preserved its silence, just as it had before Paula came back.

How had she managed to make such a difference in this place in a few short weeks? How had she managed to make such a difference in their lives? He'd told himself he no longer believed in happy endings. But Paula had begun to make a believer out of him.

If they shared many more moments like those out on the patio last night, he'd no longer have a choice about it. He'd tried, in the quiet hours of the night, to apply reason and logic to his reactions. But reason and logic didn't seem to fit the emotions Paula roused in him.

He carried his briefcase into the library, telling himself to concentrate on business. The meeting with Dieter had gone better than he'd dared hope. The man's assistant had even dropped a hint that they'd enjoy an opportunity to become acquainted with a number of community leaders—perhaps an informal social event at the Caine mansion?

Alex had quickly agreed, making mental lists to line up the caterers and have his secretary send invitations. Town council members, business owners, police chief, doctor—he'd have to include them all. Dieter and his associates wouldn't suggest such an event, he felt sure, unless they were on the verge of signing the agreement.

He heard Paula's steps sounding in the hallway. A moment later she walked into the library, and he knew moonlight had had nothing to do with his feelings.

"Paula." He rounded the table, wanting to eliminate the distance between them. "I'm glad you're here."

She stopped in the middle of the oriental carpet, reminding him of the day she'd stood there telling him he had to let her stay. She looked just as determined now as she had then.

"I need to talk with you." She seemed guarded, folding her arms across the rainbow design on the front of her T-shirt.

"That's good, because I want to talk with you, too." His news would wipe that concerned expression from her face. "About last night."

A warm flush brightened her peaches-and-cream skin, and he knew she was thinking of those moments on the patio. Suddenly he was there, holding her in his arms and wanting never to let her go.

"The dinner party," he added quickly. "I wanted to thank you for everything you did to make it a success. Dieter was pleased."

"That's nice." She shrugged her shoulders, as if to dismiss that as of no importance. "But—"

"Nice? It's more than nice." He closed the gap between them with a quick stride. "I've told you how important this deal is to the company's survival." He wanted to take her hands, but her body language set a barrier between them. "I think they're almost ready to sign."

The enthusiasm and encouragement he'd anticipated weren't there, and it annoyed him. Didn't she understand how important this was?

"They've asked for an opportunity to meet community leaders. That has to be a prelude to announcing a deal." Energy surged through him. He was going to pull this off. For an instant he imagined he'd look at the portrait of his father over the fireplace and read approval there. "I want to hold a reception here next Saturday. My secretary will take care of the invitations and schedule the catering. You'll handle it the way you did the dinner party."

Again she responded with the briefest of shrugs, as if the most important deal of his life were a trifle. "Yes, good." Her mind was obviously elsewhere.

"I'm glad it's working out, but I need to speak with you about something else."

Apparently he'd been wrong. He tried not to feel disappointment at her attitude. Paula didn't share his triumph. Apparently she didn't see this as anything more than just another job.

"What is it?" He took a step back, hearing his voice harden. "What's so important?"

"Jason." The muscles in her neck moved, as if she struggled to swallow. "I'm worried about Jason."

"Is he ill?" He glanced toward the hallway. "I assumed he was out when I didn't hear him."

"He is." She shook her head. "I mean, no, he's not ill. Rebecca picked him up to play with Kristie for the afternoon."

"Then what is it?"

"He's upset. I found him crying this morning." She hesitated, glancing away as if she didn't want to look at him. "He saw us last night. When we were on the patio. When we were kissing."

So that's what this was all about. "Paula, I'm sorry he was upset about it, but that's hardly surprising. I haven't...there hasn't been another woman in our lives since his mother left."

"It's not just that. I wish he hadn't seen us, but that's a minor part of the problem. He was genuinely upset, even angry." Color flamed in her cheeks. "He reminded me that we kissed the last time I was here. And then I went away."

Shame over Alex's behavior then reared its head, and he slammed it down. He couldn't let himself be sidetracked by past mistakes.

"Look, I know this is important, but I don't believe it's as serious as you're making out. I'll speak with Jason, explain it to him. He's a bright child, he'll understand."

Her soft mouth firmed in a stubborn line. "Alex, this is serious. You don't understand. Jason is troubled. He needs your time and attention right now."

Something in him tightened with annoyance. Paula was creating mountains out of molehills. Much as he appreciated her concern for Jason, she was letting herself get carried away. He tried reason.

"This summer hasn't been easy for Jason, I realize that. As soon as this business with Dieter is settled, I'll make more time for him. But this deal has to take priority. It will assure everyone's future, including Jason's."

She was shaking her head before he finished speaking. "Jason needs you now. He needs his father's attention."

His control slipped, and he felt himself reach for the protective barrier that was part of his Caine family tradition. "I'm doing what I have to for everyone, Paula, including Jason. I'm afraid you'll just have to accept the fact that I know best.''

Alex's arrogant words were like a match set to the tinder of her emotions, Paula realized. He knew best, according to him. Whatever was happening, whatever she thought and felt, Alex believed, just as her father always did, that he knew what was right for everyone.

"No.'' The word came out with the force of an explosion.

Alex looked at her, eyebrows lifting, perhaps at her daring to question him. "What?''

"I said no.'' She took a breath, trying to hold on to whatever composure she had left. She had to make him understand. "I'm sorry, but in this situation you don't know best. Not if you think your business deal comes before your son.''

He didn't move, but he withdrew. His frozen, superior expression told her she was losing him.

"My relationship with my son is not your concern.''

"Yes, it is.'' She tried not to think about those moments in his arms, because if she did, she'd be lost. "I care about him.'' *And about you.* "I can't just stand back and ignore it when I see him hurting.''

His dark eyes flickered, telling her that had touched him.

"I'm sorry." His voice softened. "Paula, I know you care about Jason. I shouldn't have said that. But you have to understand how important this is. The whole town will be affected by what I do in the next few days."

She knew he believed that. She could almost sense the heavy load of his responsibility for this town and its people. "Don't you see? The town needs you, yes. But not in the way your son does."

"Jason is just as affected as everyone else by the success or failure of this deal. It's his future I'm trying to assure."

He'd put up that shield that protected him from normal human emotions. She'd like to rattle him, but she knew that wasn't going to happen. Alex didn't get rattled. He'd just freeze her out, and she'd never be able to reach him.

"Is that what you think? That financial security is what Jason needs from you?"

He turned away, and despair gripped her. She looked from him to the portrait of his father, staring arrogantly out at the world as if he owned it.

"I suppose he'd approve of what you're doing?" She flung her hand out toward the painting.

Alex's jaw tightened until it looked made of marble. "My father's approval has nothing to do with this." The words were chipped from ice.

"Doesn't it?" She'd gone too far now. There was no going back. "Isn't that what this is all about, Alex? You're still trying to earn his approval, and you're doing it by repeating all of his mistakes. You're not thinking about Jason. You're thinking about the precious Caine family name!''

She stopped, suddenly breathless and exhausted. Alex stared at her as if from a very long distance. Then he walked to the library door and opened it.

It was over—that was all she could think. She walked out, passing him, trying to hold on to whatever composure she could. She'd tried to make him understand, tried to do what she thought God expected of her. And she'd failed. She wouldn't have another chance.

Chapter Fifteen

Paula's smile vanished as she closed the door of Aunt Maida's room in the rehab unit. She'd managed to maintain an air of normalcy during her visit, but she didn't think Aunt Maida had been fooled.

Leave it in God's hands, Aunt Maida had said as Paula was leaving. *Whatever the problem, leave it in God's hands.*

Unfortunately that seemed easier said than done. Paula stood for a moment, looking out at the courtyard of the rehabilitation unit, abloom with roses. She'd tried to turn her worries for Jason over to the Lord, just as she'd tried to relinquish her pain over the situation with Alex. But her rebellious spirit kept picking the burden up again. Surely there was something she could do—some way to make this right.

"Hi, Paula. How is she today?" Brett Elliot tucked a chart under his arm as he loped down the hall toward her. "Is she ready to get out of here and tackle the world?"

She had to smile, because that was an apt description of Aunt Maida's mood. "Just about. When do you think she'll be able to come home?"

"I'd like to hang on to her a few more days." He checked the chart. "Let's at least wait until after this reception Alex is planning. If we send her home before that, you'll have to tie her down to keep her from helping."

Even the most casual mention of Alex was enough to set the still-painful wound throbbing, but she managed to keep her smile on straight. "You know her too well."

"How is everything going with you?"

Brett's sympathetic tone was almost her undoing, and she struggled to suppress her worries. "I think the reception is under control." She deliberately kept the conversation superficial. He was Alex's friend, and she certainly couldn't discuss Alex with him, no matter how sympathetic he was.

"Alex tends to have a one-track mind about things like that," Brett said, his tone casual. "I've always thought he had way too much sense of responsibility. Of course, back in the old days, he said I had too little." He glanced over her shoulder. "Speaking of Alex, here he is now."

The warning gave her a moment to catch her breath and stiffen her spine before she turned.

"I didn't realize you were coming to see Maida this morning." *If I had, I wouldn't be here.*

Alex, dauntingly businesslike in a dark suit, came to a stop a few feet from them, as if he didn't want to get any closer to her than necessary.

"I had to come to town, anyway, to see an attorney about some business."

"I see." At least Brett was there, so they weren't alone.

"I'd better be off. Duty calls." Brett was halfway down the hall before she could react. "See you Saturday," he called over his shoulder, and left her alone with Alex.

Alex turned to her, and she tried to find some armor to protect her. There was something she had to say to him, if only she could get it out without betraying how she really felt.

"Brett says Aunt Maida ·can come home next week." She hoped that sounded as casual and cheerful as she wanted it to.

"Good. You can take off whatever time you need to get her settled." Alex glanced toward Maida's door, as if ready to move on at the earliest opportunity.

"I wondered…" She took a deep breath to still the quaking inside her. Was it better if his answer was yes or no? She really didn't know, so she'd better just get it out. "Once Maida is home, she might be able to supervise someone else doing the work. I'm sure we could work it out, if you'd prefer that I leave then."

He froze, but his well-bred mask didn't betray his opinion. "Is that what you want?"

Only the truth would do here, she knew. "No, it's not. If I leave now, I'll be doing the same thing I did the last time. That would just confirm Jason's fears, and I don't want to do that."

Do you? Talk to me about it, Alex. Please.

He gave a curt nod. "Fine. Stay until Maida is on her feet again." He turned toward the door. "I'll go in and see her now. Then I must get back to the plant."

It wasn't fine, but there also wasn't anything she could do about it. She'd stay until her aunt was well, and she'd try to ignore the pain that clutched her heart each time she saw Alex.

When Maida had recovered, when they'd had time to prepare Jason, she'd leave. And this time, when she left Bedford Creek, she wouldn't be coming back.

The reception spilled from the French doors as the crowd eddied through the downstairs of the mansion, out onto the sunlit lawn, across the patio. Alex made his way methodically from one group to another, encountering smiles and chatter. People seemed to be enjoying themselves, and that included the visitors from Dieter Industries.

A small group clustered around a table serving hot appetizers. He would have had the caterer set up a formal buffet in the dining room, but Paula had suggested a number of small serving stations, instead, scattered throughout the house and grounds. She'd been right. His guests mixed and reformed again and again, and Dieter's people mixed with the rest.

He scanned the crowd—men in suits, women in colorful dresses that brightened in the sunshine like so many flowers. Where was Dieter? The man had proved remarkably evasive of late. Tension formed a knot in Alex's stomach, and he deposited the mushroom tart he'd been eating on the nearest tray. He'd expected, by this time, that Dieter would have—

"Dad?" Jason, wearing a dark suit and tie that replicated his father's attire, tugged on his sleeve and looked up at him questioningly. "Did you hear me?"

"Sorry, Jason." He tried to concentrate on his son, but his gaze kept straying to the surrounding crowd. Where was Dieter, anyway? "What did you say?"

"When is Maida going to come home?" Jason's small face tightened. "You said we'd talk about it, but we never did."

"Soon." Alex patted his shoulder. "The doctor says she can come home soon."

"But when?" Jason's voice took on a whining note. "When, Dad? I want to know now."

"Jason." He swallowed the tone of exasperation. "Look, son, I don't have an exact date, not yet. But she will be back. Just trust me on this, please."

"But what about Paula? Is she going to go away? I don't want her to." Jason's lower lip came out in a pout. "I want her to stay. Make her stay, Dad."

His tension went up a notch at the mention of Paula, until his very skin seemed to tingle with it. His hand tightened on the glass he held. Paula wouldn't stay long—he was sure of that. When they'd talked earlier, she'd made her feelings clear enough. She was staying because she felt Jason and Maida both needed her, not for any other reason.

"Da-ad!" Jason's whine was loud enough to attract attention.

He frowned down at his son. "Jason, this isn't the time or place to talk about this. We'll discuss it later. Everything's going to be all right, I promise."

For a moment Jason looked as if he'd flare up at him. Then he spun away and darted through the crowd.

Alex held out his hand, but it was too late to call Jason back.

Just as it was too late for a lot of other things.

He slammed the door on that morbid thought.

He'd make this up to Jason. As soon as the deal was completed, he'd arrange a weekend trip for the two of them. He and Jason would find a way to talk the way they used to—the way he and his father never had.

Paula would see that everything he'd done was for the best. She'd see—

The crowd around him moved toward a server with a platter of chilled shrimp, the ruffle of movement creating an open path along the grass. Looking down it, he saw Paula.

His throat tightened. She looked like a daffodil in the yellow sundress she wore, and the sunlight gilded her warm skin with gold. She looked like everything he'd ever wanted in a woman—everything he wanted now and couldn't have.

The open space between them turned into a gap—a yawning chasm he didn't know how to cross. They were too far apart; they'd said too many bitter things to each other. There was no way back.

Paula stared at him what seemed a long moment. Then she turned away.

He'd wanted her to stop looking at him as if he were a hero, as if he were the prince in a fairy tale. Well, he didn't need to worry about that any longer. Now she looked at him as if he were the frog.

Paula's heart thumped painfully as she turned away from Alex. This was so difficult—so much harder than she'd dreamed it would be. Her remembered emotions for Alex had been sharp enough to hurt when she'd come back. Now the pain had intensified a hundred times.

She'd thought, or at least she'd hoped, that he'd be able to pull down the walls he held against the rest of the world. She'd imagined she could get close enough to make a difference in his life. That was clearly impossible. As far as she could tell, even Jason's mother hadn't been able to do that.

This wasn't just about what was best for Jason. If it had been that simple, there might have been a way through it. But she'd been fighting three generations' worth of Caine family tradition, and she'd lost.

It was ironic, in a way. She'd always thought her choices had been restricted by her family's working class background. Now she knew that Alex's life had been just as restricted by his family's wealth.

She made her way through the crowd, automatically checking the serving tables as she went. In one way or another, all of these people depended on Alex. That very fact set barriers between them and Alex, whether they realized it or not.

She'd reached the pool area when she realized the crowd was falling silent. Alex and Dieter, surrounded by Dieter's colleagues, stood near the gazebo, and Dieter clinked a spoon against a glass.

The businessman beamed as he held up his hands. "I wish to make a small announcement to my new friends here in Bedford Creek," he said. "I am pleased to tell you that we have come to an agreement joining Caine Industries with the Dieter Corporation in a venture we trust will bring increased prosperity to all of us."

So, Alex had done what he'd set out to do. Paula joined in the applause, trying to feel some genuine happiness for this result. Of course she was pleased. This meant a great deal to Alex personally, as well as to the town. But it was hard to join in the general celebrating when her heart hurt.

People started moving forward to offer their congratulations. Mitch and Anne got there first, closely followed by Brett with Rebecca. The sight of that close little group surrounding Alex just reminded her that she wasn't part of it. She slipped to the rear of the crowd, swallowing hard. She'd better try to get her emotions under control before she did anything else.

The housekeeper's cottage looked like a haven. She'd give a great deal to be able to go inside and close the door. But she couldn't forget she had a job to do. She had to—

She stopped, frowning. Some foreign odor mingled with the aroma of food and flowers—something vaguely unpleasant. Her stomach lurched.

Smoke! She smelled smoke, coming from the old gardener's cottage Alex used as a studio.

Quickly she hurried around the small building to the door, pulse hammering, trying to reassure herself. She must be mistaken. There wasn't anything in the studio that could be burning. And she certainly couldn't start a panic. She'd have to investigate.

She grasped the knob, relieved to find it cool to the touch. This was nothing—she was letting her imagination run away with her. Besides, the building was probably locked—

The knob turned under her hand. She yanked the door open.

Fire! Panic crashed over her, stealing her breath in an instant. Flames shot from the trash can, and the draft from the opening door sent gray smoke billowing toward her. She clenched the knob. A cry ripped from her throat in spite of her effort to keep it back.

Run, the voice screamed in her head. *Run, run!* Suddenly she was back in the plane, the flames sweeping toward her, the twisted belt trapping her in the seat. She'd never get out, she—

Then she saw something that cut through her nightmare like a knife. The half-finished carving of Jason, covered by its cloth, sat on the workbench. Next to it lay the design plans Alex had shown her. Almost against her will, her mind assessed the risk.

They weren't in danger yet, but if the curtains caught, if she waited for help to arrive...

The fire extinguisher hung from a hook just inside the door. A prayer for help echoing in her heart, she grabbed the metal canister and advanced on the flames.

Please, God. Please. She wasn't trapped in the past any longer. A shudder ripped through her, but she shook it off. She wouldn't give in to the fear. With God's help, she never would again.

Chapter Sixteen

The moment Alex heard the cry, he knew it was Paula. Not stopping to wonder at the certainty that propelled him, he pushed his way through the crowd, ignoring their astonished stares. Paula was in trouble.

An acrid smell assaulted him as he rounded the pool. His stomach lurched. *Smoke!* He raced toward the studio, heart pounding, throat tight. Something was on fire, and Paula was there. She'd be terrified. He had to get to her.

The cottage door stood open. Gray smoke funneled out into the clean air. Behind him he could hear calls as others realized what was happening.

"Alex, wait!" It was Mitch's voice.

He couldn't wait. Paula was inside, maybe

trapped, flames reaching toward her—past and present mixed in a dizzying, terrifying scenario.

He ran to the door, throwing his arm up to shield his face, and stumbled inside. "Paula!"

She swung at the sound of his voice. Not trapped. Not terrified. Foam dripped from the extinguisher she held over the trash can. Even as he watched, the last wisps of smoke dissipated.

His mind seemed one huge prayer of thanks. She was all right. He went to her quickly, taking the metal canister from her hands.

"Are you hurt?" He clasped her hands in his, wanting to pull her into his arms, but not quite daring.

Paula nodded, coughing a little. "It's out. I put it out." Something like wonder filled her eyes as she looked at him. "I put it out," she repeated.

"You certainly did." He felt a long shudder work through her, and his hands slipped to her arms. Again he wanted to pull her against him. But heavy footsteps pounded on the porch, and the small room suddenly filled with people.

"Paula, how do you feel? Any trouble breathing?" Brett brushed past, elbowing him out of the way, intent on Paula. Mitch knelt by the soot-covered trash can. He picked it up gingerly and started toward the door.

Alex stepped back. His heartbeat should go back to normal now that the crisis was over, but that didn't seem to be happening. "Why didn't you call me?" He broke into Brett's series of questions. "You should have gotten out of here. You should have let someone else handle it."

Paula glanced toward the table, toward the carving of Jason. "I couldn't wait. I couldn't risk losing that." She looked back at him, and it felt as if no one else was in the room.

"Paula…" He let the sentence trail away. They were talking to each other without the need for words. They both knew what had just happened, whether anyone else did or not. Paula had faced the thing that terrified her most in this world, and she'd done it to save something important to him. His throat closed, and all he could do was look at her and think how dear she was to him.

"How did it start?" Mitch frowned at the remnants in the can. "I wouldn't think there'd be anything to spark a fire in here."

Alex tried to pull his gaze away from Paula. "It doesn't matter," he began, then became aware of a small figure in the doorway. *Jason.* His son shouldn't be exposed to this. It might frighten him. "Jason—"

"It was me!" Jason's face was white. "It was my fault. All my fault!"

Alex didn't know which of them moved first. He and Paula got to Jason at the same time. "No, Jason, no. It's not your fault, son. Don't think that."

Jason jerked away from his hand. "It is," he insisted almost angrily. "I did it."

Alex could only stare at the boy, totally at a loss.

"You were playing with matches." Paula said it softly, so softly probably no one else heard. "Is that what happened?"

A denial rose in Alex's throat, but before he could speak, Jason nodded. His small face crumpled.

"I'm sorry, Daddy. I didn't mean to. I'm sorry."

"Jason..." He stopped, reading the clear message in Paula's gaze. *Hold him.* She might as well have said it aloud. This wasn't the moment for analyzing or arguing. Alex knelt on the sooty floor. Feeling as if his heart might break, he drew his son into his arms.

For an instant Jason seemed to resist, then he flung his arms around Alex's neck, clinging as he hadn't in years. Sobs shook him.

"It's all right," Alex murmured, stroking his child's back. "It's all right, Jason."

His gaze met Paula's over Jason's head. The sheen of tears brightened her eyes.

"Is something wrong? What is happening?"

Dieter's voice had to be one of the most unwelcome things Alex had ever heard, when only moments before it had seemed so important. Aware of Paula watching him, he glanced up, not relaxing his grip on his son.

"Just a small accident," he said. His gaze caught Mitch's. "Would you?" He jerked his head toward Dieter.

Mitch nodded, not needing any further explanation. "Everything's under control now, folks." He began ushering people toward the patio, his large frame protecting Jason from curious eyes. "Let's get back to the party."

A murmur of voices, the shuffle of feet, and they were gone. Beside him, he felt Paula move, too.

"I should go. "

He shook his head. "Stay. Please." He stroked Jason's hair, his hand unsteady. "We need you, Paula."

That was as true as anything he'd ever said. He needed her. He loved his son more than life itself, but he didn't know how to reach him. If he didn't do this right, he'd probably regret it the rest of his days.

Please, Lord. Please. The prayer was almost involuntary. How long had it been since he'd begged God on his knees? The thought startled him. He'd been raised to be self-reliant. Somehow that attitude had extended to his faith, almost without his realizing it.

Paula nodded, seeming to understand all the things Alex didn't say. She moved closer, touching Jason's shoulder.

"Jason, it's okay. I understand."

Jason burrowed against his father's neck, and his voice was muffled. "I promised you."

"You didn't mean to break your promise," she said.

Her voice stayed calm, and Alex could only guess at the effort it took. He wanted to demand answers, but this wasn't the time. He could only try to understand.

"Tell your daddy what happened," she said gently. "He won't be angry."

Jason shook his head.

"Come on," she coaxed. "Were you mad?"

Jason sniffled. "Everybody was busy with this dumb party." A sob interrupted his words. "I just wanted someone to pay attention to me."

Someone. The word rang in Alex's mind. He remembered that exchange with Jason, how he'd brushed off his son's worries in his own anxiety over the business deal.

"So you were playing with matches in here." Her gaze ordered Alex not to react.

He felt Jason's nod, and then finally Jason raised his head, his gaze searching Alex's face. "I'm sorry, Daddy. I didn't mean to start a fire. I guess one of the matches wasn't clear out when I threw it away. I didn't mean it."

Alex gently wiped away the tears on Jason's face. "Fires are pretty scary, aren't they."

Jason nodded again, and his lips trembled. "I'm

sorry. I just needed to know. About Maida, and Paula, and everything.''

"I know, son. I'm sorry, too. But..." He censored the automatic response that assured Jason not to worry. Obviously that did no good. Jason did worry, whether Alex wanted him to or not. "You know I love you, don't you?"

"Mommy loved me." The words burst out, as if Jason had been holding them in for a long time. "Mommy loved me, but she went away. It was my fault."

"Jason, no. Why would you think that?" Appalled, he could only stare at his son, feeling his heart shatter into pieces.

Jason hung his head, staring at the floor. He sniffled a little. "I wasn't good enough. That's why she went away."

How was he going to find the words? His son's pain wrapped around his heart, squeezing the life out of it.

Please, God. I've tried so hard to be the perfect heir my father wanted, but I've failed my own son. Please. Help me.

Paula watched the battle on Alex's face. His torment showed in his eyes so clearly. If he realized how much he was giving away, would he shut down again? Shut her out?

Alex stroked Jason's cheek. "Jason, that's not it

at all. Of course your mommy loved you, more than anything. If she could have come back, I'm sure she would have. It wasn't your fault she went away. Mommy and I just couldn't seem to get along together. We made each other unhappy.''

A strong fist seemed to grip her heart. Alex was opening up to his son. Maybe for the first time, he was being vulnerable to the boy.

Please, Father, don't let him pull back now. Help him to tear down the barriers between them.

Jason shook his head as if he couldn't let go of the responsibility. He and Alex were so alike in that quality, and Alex had never seen it.

''Yes,'' Alex insisted. ''Don't you remember how she used to sing you to sleep at night?''

''She did?'' That simple idea seemed to break through Jason's absorption.

''Sure she did—''

Alex glanced at Paula, as if looking for confirmation he was on the right track, and she nodded, smiling through the tears that insisted on falling.

''And she made you that little stuffed dog that's on your dresser.''

Jason stared into his father's face. ''But she went away.''

''I know.'' She saw the muscles work in Alex's jaw. ''I'm sorry I didn't talk to you about it more. I guess I thought you were too little to understand.''

Jason straightened. "I'm big enough, Dad. I want to know what's going on."

"I see that now." Alex stood, holding out his hand to Jason. "Let's sit down and talk about it, okay?"

"Okay." Jason tucked his small hand into Alex's.

As father and son moved toward the bench against the wall, Paula slipped quietly out the door. Alex was doing it. He was taking down, stone by stone, the wall that separated him from his son. He could do that now without her.

She hesitated when she reached the patio. Snatches of conversation reached her ears, and the flurry of excitement was clearly over. Mitch stood on the pool deck, casually talking with someone, but his position was such that no one could go past him toward the studio. Brett had corralled several of Dieter's deputies near the gazebo, and Anne seemed to be keeping Dieter himself occupied.

She couldn't go back to the party, not until the last traces of tears were gone from her face. She moved softly across the grass and behind the shelter of the yew hedge.

The buzz of conversation turned into the merest background noise, quieter than the twittering of wrens in the hedge. Peace filled her.

Thank you, Lord. She glanced up, toward the

mountain ridge cutting into the sky. *Thank you. I think I understand now.*

She and Alex were more alike than she'd thought. He'd been trying to prove he was the perfect Caine heir his father wanted. She'd thought she had to earn the approval her father had never given. The truth was that neither of them had to prove their value in God's sight. They were accepted, just the way they were.

She wiped away another tear. She wasn't the starstruck girl she'd been two years ago, who ran away from rejection and told herself she didn't need anyone. She'd like to believe that, if not for the loss of her memory, she'd have dealt with that failing long ago, but this was her chance. Perhaps this had been in Aunt Maida's mind all along, when she'd pushed Paula into the situation. This time she wouldn't run away, no matter how difficult the future might be.

She loved Alex. If he didn't care for her in the same way, if the differences between them were too great, she'd deal with that. But she wouldn't run away from it.

"Paula."

She turned at the sound of Alex's voice, her heart thudding. "Is Jason all right?"

He nodded. "He will be. Thanks to you."

"I didn't do anything." Her throat was tight with

longing. "You're the one he needed." *The one I need.*

Alex shook his head. "I'd never have known that without you. I'd have kept on trying to protect him, not realizing I was closing him out." He moved closer. "You understood me better than I understood myself. If I succeed in being a better father, it will be because of you."

"I'm glad." She knew the love she felt for him was shining in her eyes, but she couldn't help it. There weren't any walls between them, at least not any of her making. Whether Alex could say the same, she didn't know.

His step closed the distance between them. He stood very close, not touching. "I don't think I'll ever be the perfect father I wanted to be."

"Jason doesn't need a perfect father. He needs you." It was much the same thing she'd said when he'd rejected the idea that he was a hero.

Perhaps he remembered that, because he smiled. "Not a hero," he said quietly. "Not a perfect father. Are you willing to take a chance on someone as fallible as I am?"

Her heart seemed to stop beating for a moment as she looked up into his eyes. It took a moment to find the words. "I've always been ready to take a chance. And in case you haven't noticed, I'm not so perfect myself."

He drew her into his arms, and she was home.

She rested her cheek against his chest and felt the steady beating of his heart.

"Will you marry me, Paula?" His breath stirred her hair. "Will you stay with us forever?"

She looked up at him, seeing the love so strong in his dark eyes that it took her breath away. Maybe they weren't perfect, but with God's help they could build a family that would last.

"I will."

He pressed his cheek against hers, and her heart overflowed. God had poured blessings on them, and all they'd had to do was open their hearts and hands. From now on the memories they made would be ones they could share, with God's grace.

*   *   *   *   *

Dear Reader,

I'm so glad you decided to pick up this book. The love story of small-town millionaire Alex Caine and his reluctant housekeeper, Paula Hansen, is one that has been teasing my imagination for a long time. I'm delighted to see it in print, and I hope you'll enjoy it.

Alex is the kind of person who thinks he has to be perfect for everyone, including God. It takes a near disaster to make him see the truth—that God's acceptance is already won for him. Once he understands that, he's finally ready for the happily-ever-after he always thought was an illusion. And he finds it in the surprise Cinderella who's right there in his own house.

Please let me know how you liked this story. You can reach me c/o Steeple Hill Books, 300 East 42nd St., New York, NY 10017.

Best wishes,

Marta Perry

Next month from Steeple Hill's

Love Inspired

A SPECIAL KIND
OF FAMILY
by

Eileen Berger

*After her grandmother breaks her hip,
Vanessa McHenry takes charge of the five
pregnant teenagers in Granny's care. The
local community, including old boyfriend
Rob Corland, pitches in to help. Soon
Vanessa rediscovers her faith in God—
and her love for Rob.*

**Don't miss
A SPECIAL KIND OF FAMILY
On sale March 2001**